TERROR IN THE TRENCH: AN AQUATIC HORROR ANTHOLOGY

"Terror in the Trench": Volume One of the *Dead Seas* series. An aquatic horror anthology from Dead Sea Press. Featuring stories from Laurel Hightower, Kay Hanifen, Mocha Pennington, Joshua Marsella, Thomas Gloom, Nicola Kapron, Nikki R. Leigh, Spencer Hamilton, Matthew Stevens, Megan Kiekel Anderson, Andrew Cull, Catarina Prata, Hannah Hulbert, Craig Wallwork, and Jack Harding.

First edition published March 2022 by Dead Sea Press.

All profits from the sale of this book will go directly to The Shark Trust, registered charity number 1064185. Check our website bloodriteshorror.com/dsp to see how much we've raised.

TRADE PAPERBACK ISBN: 978-1-915272-07-2

Edited by Jay Alexander.

The characters, scenes and situations in this book are fictional and any likeness to those in the real world is coincidental. Where historical figures and events have been cited, those figures and events are representations that exist solely within the *Dead Seas* universe.

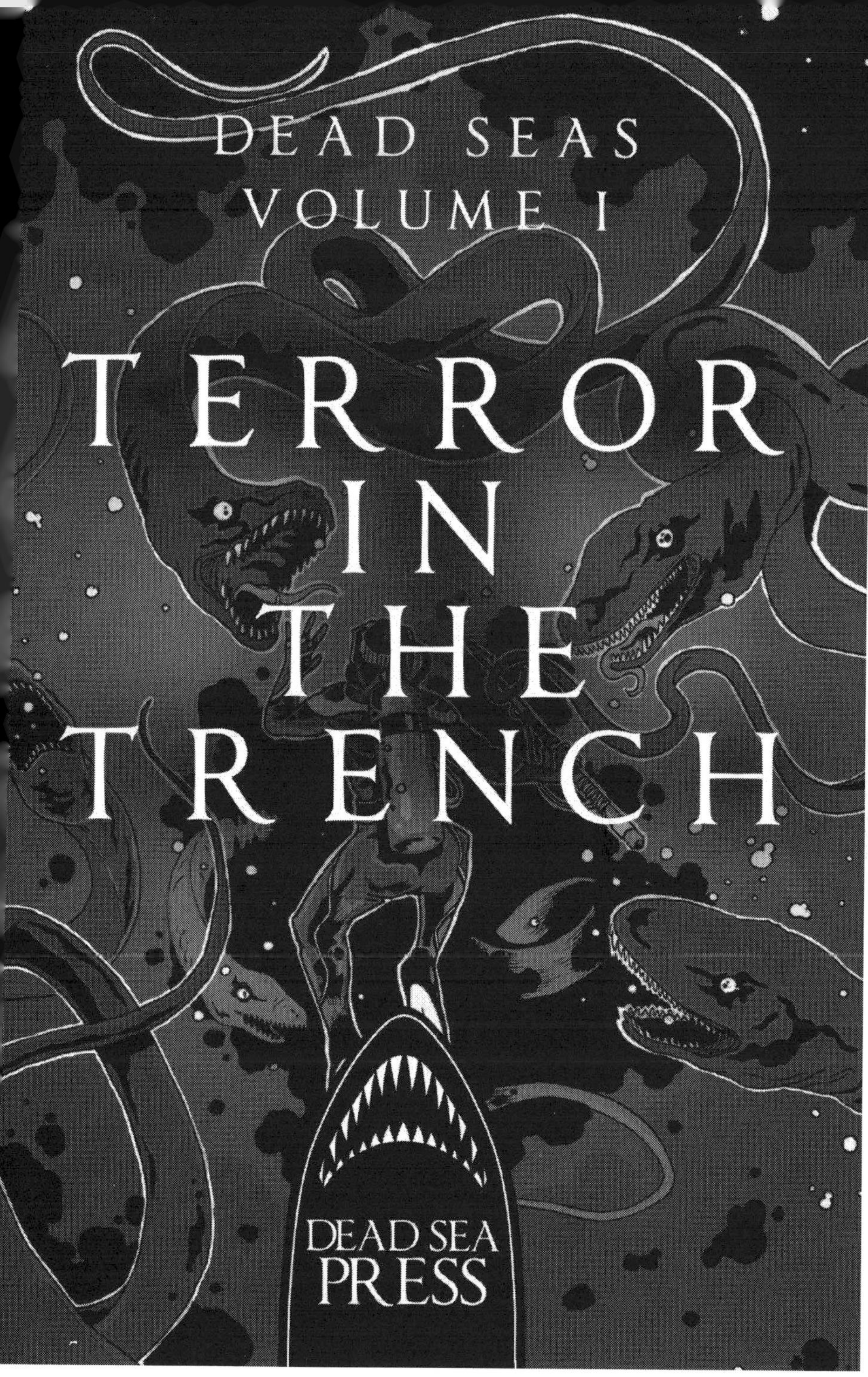
DEAD SEAS
VOLUME I
TERROR
IN
THE
TRENCH
DEAD SEA
PRESS

100% of the profits from sales of this book will be donated to The Shark Trust (registered charity number 1064185) in support of their continued efforts to protect and conserve sharks and other oceanic wildlife.

Thank you for purchasing a copy and helping to support the hard work of the Shark Trust team, and the amazing creatures they aim to protect.

CONTENT WARNINGS

The stories in this book are works of horror fiction and may contain scenes of graphic violence, threat and terror.

For detailed content warnings regarding each story, please see the very back of the book. Beware of spoilers.

CONTENTS

INTRODUCTION
BY JAY ALEXANDER

The ghost pipefish, or *Solenostomus*, is a genus of six (currently recognised) species that can be found in Indo-Pacific waters. They eat minute crustaceans, ingesting them by floating almost motionlessly with their mouths pointed downward, and have been around since the Eocene—upwards of thirty million years ago. The ghost pipefish has a head that makes up for forty-four per cent of its entire body size.

You probably know that sharks can grow their teeth back, many species for most of their lives. Did you know that this is because they are, essentially, closer to scales?

Did you know that crabs have tastebuds on their feet? Or that the sting of a stonefish is believed to be the most painful a human can experience? Or, indeed, that a hatched baby octopus is smaller than your pinky finger?

Did you know that, while sharks are believed to kill less than twenty humans per year, we, as a species, kill 11,500 sharks per *hour*?

The ocean is a fascinating, terrifying, endlessly vast and endlessly beautiful place. There are more creatures in the ocean than we could ever imagine, and so many more that we have yet to discover. It is often compared to space, with its unknowable expanses of wonderful, weird and incredible life, but whereas space is so very far removed from our daily experience, one only has to dip a toe into the ocean to get a feeling of that ever-reaching blue, that ever-living and moving and uncontrollably brilliant world so full of kaleidoscopic and contorting colours—to get a sense of just how much is *out there*.

Make no mistake: this is a collection of horror stories. *Terror in the Trench* brings together fifteen tales of oceanic monsters, of ghostly apparitions upon the waves, of death and ungodliness and vast, leviathan jaws snapping shut. But I should like also for it to serve as a reminder of the strength and beauty of the sea, and one of our duty to protect it.

Why even try, you might ask, to represent the oceans as a force and power and wonderful way of life to be saved and respected with *horror*, a genre that can only paint the creatures—supernatural, otherworldly, or as real as you and I—as monstrous and terrifying? Ever since *Jaws* gave film lovers an image of a shark that is destructive and furious, that is hungry and vengeful, horror and Hollywood have played their own part in wrongfully conveying the beasts of the ocean. Even Peter Benchley, upon discovering a swathe of finned shark corpses, discarded carelessly on the seabed on one of his dives, spoke out about the negative impact his book and the resulting film had had.

We aim to change this. To publish horror stories that not only thrill and frighten, but encourage you to consider the real power of the ocean and her "monsters". Go into this book remembering just that: that these creatures are not all they seem, that they are often misunderstood, and that they *need our help*.

100% of the profits from sales of this book will be donated to The Shark Trust, a UK-based charity working to promote the conservation of sharks, skates and rays. This is just one of the fantastic charities we at Dead Sea Press hope to support in the coming months and years, and their work is so important, not just to me personally but to the entire system by which all life on Earth is bound. To you, I extend my deepest gratitude; by simply owning a copy of this book, you have helped to make a difference. And while you will be informed—constantly—of the horrors lurking out there in the vast depths of the *Dead Seas* universe, I would urge you to see the beauty in the horror you're about to read.

It's about time to throw you in the deep end, I think, dear, unsuspecting reader. It would, however, be horribly remiss of me to introduce this book without mentioning the authors involved.

The Dead Sea Press inbox has been a consistent source of motivation for me in the last couple of months. I have always been convinced that horror, as a genre, can not only betray or squeeze, but reveal and strengthen the human heart in equal measure—it's a genre that touches people's truest emotions, that makes honest fears and feelings, secret phobias and guilty pleasures. It has been, I've found, one of the deepest wells—or trenches, I suppose—of *soul* that one can enter. Combing through submissions for the first three anthologies in the *Dead Seas* series (the first of which, of course, you hold in your hands right now), I discovered such a tremendous outpouring of love and support for the cause these books were designed to contribute toward, such a devastatingly powerful bounty of passion and spirit for the work that was being presented to me, that I knew almost immediately this would be the project I've been proudest of so far in my career.

Anthologies, as a rule, are a terrible risk to run. Not every reader will love every story; indeed, only a very small portion will enjoy this book from start to finish. Such is the nature of collecting entries from different authors, in different styles; to assume that they will all be loved by the entirety of the readership is to boldly step your bare foot on the back of a sea cucumber and come away unscathed. However… however.

However, what you are about to read is a collection of some of the finest nautical and aquatic horror stories that I, personally, have ever had the pleasure and privilege of reading. The opportunity to see so many over the last few weeks, and the heartbreaking reality that I couldn't print them all, are two of the things that prove what I have always suspected of horror: it can really make you feel things. In *Terror in the Trench*, you'll experience fifteen of those stories, fifteen tales of expeditions to the deepest points of the ocean—or, in some cases, journeys *upward* of the things that dwelled there prior—fifteen examples of aquatic horror that it was an absolute honour to compile. If you enjoy these stories, I encourage you to take a look at the *Authors* section at the back of the book, where you'll find more information about each of the incredibly talented writers featured, as well as where to find them. A huge thank you goes out to all fifteen—it's been humbling not only to work with some of the big and growing names in the horror community of recent years, but new and climbing talents that it's an absolute thrill to print, some for the first time.

With that, I really must open the hatch and let out some of the terrible creatures that have been waiting so eagerly within this sunken wreck. I hope you enjoy, and remember to read this book a good few feet above sea level…

Jay Alexander
February 2022

DISTRESS CALL

BY LAUREL HIGHTOWER

The deck of the risen submarine pitched in the waves beside Sophie's vessel, silent and dark. Its name was painted in blocky letters on the side—the USS *Ligeia*. A Gato-class submarine commissioned in December 1940, it had disappeared from radar in early 1942. It was presumed sunk, and based on the accumulation of algae that coated the sides of the ship, this seemed a likely explanation for its seventy-eight-year absence.

Except, that didn't explain how it had suddenly made it to the surface again. Sophie wasn't sure, but based on the photo and video documentation she'd seen of similarly-aged wrecks, the *Ligeia* seemed in better shape than it should be. She damned sure wasn't going in the water to check below surface, but every part that she could see was complete; rusted, but not compromised. It seemed impossible, but it appeared that even after all this time on the bottom of the ocean, the damned thing was still seaworthy.

It shouldn't be. She'd said it at least twenty times since she and her employer, Rick Atlas, had followed the distress call and found the sub. The ghost ship. Once he'd gotten a look, checked the database and discovered what they were dealing with, she'd insisted over and over again that it wasn't possible. That was what she was here for—to act as Rick's voice of reason. He didn't have one himself, as he'd be the first to cheerfully admit. Your classic rich adventurer, with no perception of danger. More likeable than that description implied, but still. He'd laughed at her concerns, reminded her what a find they had on their hands, and ventured into darkness through a hatch that hadn't been opened for nearly eighty years.

That had been forty minutes ago. Sophie stared through the gaping maw into the belly of the submarine, dark and empty as it had been each time she'd checked. Rick should have been back by now, no question. She hadn't been able to raise him on the radio, but he'd warned her that might be the case.

"The double hull could interfere with our signal, so don't panic if you can't get me. No need to call in the Coast Guard," he'd said.

"At what point *should* I request rescue, sir?"

He'd grinned and patted her cheek. "When we need it." He'd lowered himself from the side of his yacht and found his footing easily on the main walking deck.

"You worry too much, Soph," he'd called to her, just before disappearing from view.

She knew she did, which was why she hadn't panicked when Rick's twenty-minute timeline had passed. Or at least, she'd kept her panic on the inside and not keyed the mike to call for assistance. Instead she'd given him thirty minutes, and then forty. She could see that kind of lapse, double the time he thought he'd need, especially if manoeuvring below decks was complicated. Or if he'd seen something shiny, she thought irritably.

Anything beyond forty minutes though, she knew she'd need to investigate. And it was past time for that. The sky was growing dark as thunderheads rolled in. They'd need to get back on board the *Orchid* and to a safe distance from the sub before the ocean got too heavy.

"*Orchid* to Rick, please respond. *Orchid* to Rick, can you give me a fucking answer?"

Of course not. It was doubtful he'd even noticed he was out of contact, and if he had, he was probably glad to get a reprieve.

She stepped closer to the edge, leaned over as far as she dared. "Rick?" she called, trying hard to project her voice down the hatch. She received no answer.

"Fuck." She fought the feeling of dread—Rick paid her well to watch his back, in whatever scenario he created for himself. She owed it to him to suck it up and follow him. She called in her coordinates to the nearest Coast Guard vessel as a precaution. She used to feel silly doing it, but everyone on these waters knew Rick Atlas, and none of them would be surprised that he might require the occasional rescue. Mindful of her instructions, she'd omitted any mention of the sub, figuring it must be obvious to anyone finding the *Orchid* where they'd gone.

"Fine," she said to no one, and lowered herself to the deck of the *Ligeia.* "I've got this, no problem."

As she did, she heard the sputter of the radio above, and relief made her knees go wobbly. "About time, you asshole," she muttered, pulling herself back up and heading to the mike. "Rick? You forget how to read a watch?"

It wasn't Rick, but a repeat of the distress call they'd followed earlier. They'd tried responding, but receiving no answer, Rick had assumed it was something automated. That it hadn't been able to break the surface while the ship lay at the bottom, but now that it was topside again, the call was transmitting. But why now? What was triggering it? Was it on a loop of some kind? She knew there couldn't be anyone left on board, but it made her uneasy.

After several more minutes with no answer, she dropped back to the *Ligeia.* The skies were darker now, the waves rougher, and the gangway was soaked.

She held her breath as she entered the escape hatch

and shined her light down the ladder that led into the main portion of the sub. She could make out nothing beneath, not even whether she'd be descending into waist-deep water. Surely though, Rick would have already returned if he'd been unable to penetrate far. It had to be walkable.

"So walk it," she told herself, holding the flashlight between her teeth as she descended the ladder.

The light from above disappeared faster than she could have imagined. Before her feet hit the deck below, she was enveloped in darkness. That she could understand, but the sudden silence was eerie. The sounds of the sea above weren't just muffled, they were gone. She had the feeling of hands reaching for her from below, waiting to pull her from the ladder, and she accelerated her descent, breathless by the time she stepped off the last rung.

She shined her light throughout the tight compartment she found herself in. She'd expected to see walls of control panels; an obvious periscope sight. This was a cramped corridor that led to a set of bunks to her right, and darkness to her left.

She frowned as the beam of her flashlight caught something metallic past the bunks. Moving slow, she wondered if those bunks were occupied by the remains of the missing sailors. Her skin crawled at the idea of being trapped below sea level in a tin can filled with dead bodies.

Not exactly their choice, Sophie, she told herself. It wouldn't be the first time she'd found remains in her current employment, and she tried to keep her empathy intact. These sailors had families, loved ones who'd never known their fates.

Yet, when she passed the narrow bunks and found them all empty, somehow that was worse.

She stood staring at the grouping of gold tubes that made up the far wall. No, not gold. Brass. Torpedo tubes, she realized. Weird to see them up close, in person. Why had she always thought of them as cartoonish, not something belonging in the real world?

A clanging in the corridor behind brought her swinging around, her heart rate shooting up. "Rick?" she shouted. "That you?"

She'd expected the words to echo through the empty sub, but instead they were swallowed by the silence that pressed down on her. No wonder Rick hadn't heard her before—it was like being wrapped in cotton. He'd probably just lost track of the time and was off exploring. At least she didn't have to wonder which way to go—there was only one possibility, short of being launched out of one of those tubes.

It should have been a funny thought, but she had an image of herself wedged into one, in the dark, unable to catch her breath, and she shuddered.

"Lighten up, Sophie. This isn't *Looney Tunes*; no one's going to stuff you in a torpedo tube."

She raised the light, ready to follow it along the corridor Rick must have taken, and screamed when it illuminated a face, no more than ten feet away.

She didn't drop the flashlight, thank God, but when she swung it back to where she'd seen the face, it was gone. She stood there breathing hard, knowing it hadn't been Rick. It was a strange face, grey and blotchy, with eyes that had shone silver in the flash. Was there someone else down here? Had they done something to Rick? And where the fuck had they gone?

She looked in each of the bunks, but they remained empty. She spun in a circle, stabbing each corner with the light, but found no one in its shaky glow. She stood still and listened, but still that silence pressed down upon her.

Was it possible they weren't the first ones to find this vessel? Maybe there was a good explanation for why the damned thing had surfaced after all this time. An undersea salvage team, maybe? But then why hadn't they revealed themselves when Rick had first climbed down?

A hollow thudding sounded from somewhere up ahead, as though someone were knocking at the hull. Sophie's imagination immediately conjured an image of a Great White stalking her in the gloomy depths; an ocean full of hungry, dead-eyed carnivores. She shook it off. Nothing short of explosives was going to breach that hull.

Two more steps and she stopped again, another sound reaching her from far away. Music. It was faint, and at first she thought she'd imagined it, the way you hear a song sometimes in the hum of traffic or the scream of a hairdryer. But no, it was definitely music. Something low, with minor chords. A recording? Still playing after all this time, in an empty ghost ship? Or Rick screwing around with his cell phone? She keyed her handheld. "Rick?" she said softly, reluctant to make too much noise. There was no answer, but the strange melody began to emit from the speaker of her radio as well. She wrestled an urge to throw the damned thing. It had to be Rick.

She needed to know, and not just to solve the mystery. There was something about the music that pulled her forward, made her want to hear it better, learn enough to make it hers. That was how Sophie always found music—ambient and out in the world, waiting for her to chase its tail.

She stepped forward, moving her light back and forth in slow arcs, trying to cover all the dark corners, but that wasn't possible. She was surrounded by dark, and kept stopping every few seconds when she thought she saw something out of the corner of her eye. She passed through the engine rooms, and the crew's quarters with more of those empty bunks, but when she stepped over the threshold into what must have been the crew's mess, her foot plunged into icy water up to her shin.

She drew back with a gasp, her grip tightening on the flashlight as she shone it at the black surface. Her breath came faster when she realized the water only got deeper. It was slopping over into the crew's quarters, back the direction she'd come, and she had to clamp tight on her panic.

"Rick?" she called again, hoping like hell he'd shout back so she didn't have to wade into that blackness, but there was no answer. Just the music, which had grown no louder, and she didn't know how that was possible.

She looked back the way she'd come, at nothing but impenetrable darkness, and it gave her a jolt to realize how complete it was. She hadn't passed under any light coming from the open hatch as she'd come back by the ladder. Did that mean the storm had darkened the sky? Or that the hatch had been shut?

"Has to be the storm," she whispered out loud, an attempt to force herself calm. She shone the light into the crew's mess once more, at the choppy surface of the water that awaited her. Why the fuck had she only donned her short wetsuit? It ended well above her knees and would provide no protection from the freezing water at this depth. Were there things in it? The skeletal bodies of the lost crewmen? Or worse: things that still lived. Unnatural ocean creatures that haunted the deepest depths, brought up by the sub's ascension?

"You should be writing horror, dumbass, if all you're

going to do is make things worse," she told herself. Rick was counting on her. She couldn't pretend anymore that everything was okay—he should have been able to hear her, and if the water level was rising, it almost certainly meant he was in trouble. She switched channels and tried reaching the Coast Guard again, but there was nothing but more of that music. She frowned. That couldn't be – she must be out of range, with the transmission looping back on her. She couldn't wait on rescue, so she gritted her teeth and stepped both feet into the water, her flesh freezing up to her knees.

She kicked along at a slow pace, hoping to warn off or knock away anything that might be lurking. A couple of times she squeaked when her foot made contact with something in the invisible depths, but nothing ever came back for more, so she assumed it was the usual detritus of human occupancy. She had nearly made it to the next divider when she heard something splash behind her. Something big.

She screamed and jumped for the door, tripping over it and landing face first in the deeper water of the next compartment. She dropped the flashlight, searching frantically for it as soon as she realized what she'd done, but the murky light shone from below for only a second or two. In the momentary illumination, she found herself staring down into a face, inches below the surface. The same strange, grey complexion as the first one; the same staring, silver eyes. Then the light winked out.

Sophie spluttered and splashed, giving in fully to the panic. At first she pushed away, scrambling for distance from that awful staring face. Then logic returned. There was no one there; the image had to have been conjured by the dark and her own fear. Or, worst case, it was one of the doomed sailors, which was hardly unexpected. And face or not, she needed that fucking flashlight.

She edged forward on her hands and knees, sweeping her hands along the grated floor. The water was up to her shoulders. She looked behind her, recalling that splash and feeling exposed as hell, but she could see nothing at all.

She forced herself to keep looking for the flashlight—it was waterproof and heavy duty, and the most likely reason it had gone off was that the switch had been pressed when it hit the bottom. "Find the flashlight, you'll be fine," she told herself, bracing for the touch of cold, dead flesh. She kept herself on task by sheer force of will.

Until her fingers passed over a thick hide of scales.

She screamed again and propelled herself backward, but there was no telling herself it wasn't what it felt like. It had moved beneath her hand and she'd felt the powerful muscles of something very big.

"Oh, Jesus," she said, her teeth chattering as she pressed herself against a wall that bristled with dials and switches. The control room, had to be. So that meant she was close to the prow, and hopefully to Rick. She tried not to think about what it meant for him that something large and scaly was sharing the darkness with them.

“Rick!” she screamed. “Rick!”

Nothing, except that music. Still playing, so that had to mean Rick was okay, right? She peered into the darkness ahead and realised there was a red glow coming from somewhere up there. It was big enough for the light to reach her back here and just barely illuminate the black surface of the water.

There was no question of her next move. She couldn’t go back, not without her flashlight and with whatever had splashed into the officer’s quarters bchind her. Up ahead was light and music, and almost certainly her dumbass boss. Even if they were both in trouble, she wouldn’t be alone anymore. She just had to make her way through the dark with whatever giant fucking scaly thing shared the water with her and not get eaten. Never mind how unlikely it was that some enormous sea creature could have swum its way into the sealed submarine—the damn thing was there. She could still feel the scrape of its scales against her fingers.

It was deep enough now that swimming was actually quicker, so she set out as fast as she could for the dark portal to the next compartment. Crew’s quarters, if she remembered the schematics correctly, and she dared to hope the water might level off when it had more places to go. When something brushed against her hip she struck out crazily, scrambling to her feet and lunging over the threshold, where—thank God—the water level dropped to just over her ankles. She'd been right, she thought, bracing herself against the wall beside her. The water had made its way into the quarters of the long-dead officers.

Just a little further, that was all. She didn't let herself think about what would happen if Rick was dead when she got there. She kept following the music, the deep red glow. The strange, discordant underlying layer she now recognized as the distress beacon, somehow woven in among the other notes. That made no sense, but none of this did.

In the corridor behind her, a compartment door creaked open. She wanted, so badly, to believe it was her boss, but when she turned to look, a sailor stood behind her. His face was grey, blotchy, the flesh sloughing off around his mouth, his nose an empty hole. His eyes glowed a dead silver, and as she looked, Sophie saw that silver eyes glowed from each compartment door. The officers, at least, had not vanished aboard this ghost ship.

They began to move toward her, but their gaits were slow and strange. Her gaze ran down the body of the man closest to her, and she realized his uniform became something else, just below his hips. Thick, heavy scales covered what should have been his legs, which themselves seemed to have fused together. His upper body surged forward, his lower trailing behind, dragging a dark, ragged tail behind him. As Sophie stared, his rotting mouth opened wide, and the music she'd been following filled the room.

For a moment, she was almost lost to it. She stared into that gaping maw, with rows upon rows of teeth, all curved inward like a python's, and she didn't move at all. The music filled her heart and calmed her, and she wondered why she could never catch the words. Then the wretched stench of the dead man's breath knocked her loose from the enchantment, and she turned and ran.

One last compartment, and this was it. The fore torpedo room, she realized, with bunks the same as in the aft room. The polished brass gleamed in the unholy red light, glowing from above each one. The water had grown deep again, up to her thighs, and looking down she found it crowded with dead, staring faces.

She didn't let herself look too closely, didn't let herself count the carnage. What she did see, before her brain closed it off, was that many of them had limbs with gnawed edges, flesh torn and marrow sucked. Many of them also wore uniforms, the same as the creatures that were slowly following her into this death trap. Still more dead men lined the walls of the room, staring and silent.

There was nowhere left to go. Sophie was stuck, here among the remains of crewmen that shouldn't be here.

Men who had died to appease the appetite of whatever their shipmates had become. The same creatures who were crowding in behind her, each with that same unnatural movement of thrust, then drag. She kept backing up until she felt the press of the torpedo tube behind her. It clanged, the door having been opened somehow in the ship's unknowable lifespan. The eyes of the dead men lining the walls followed the sound, and she shuddered. She'd liked it better when she thought they couldn't move.

She glanced behind her at the tube. Would she fit in the damn thing? Claustrophobia made her chest tighten, but something big brushed against her in the standing water.

She pulled herself up, thrust herself into the darkness feet first, and scrambled to close the hatch behind her. She clutched it, sightless in the pitch black, and wondered how much time she had bought herself. Could she hold out here until the Coast Guard came to investigate? How long before they could get here, given the weather conditions? And where the hell was Rick? Was he lost amid the others, the meat torn from his bones, just another ghost to haunt the doomed submarine? Or was he in his own tube, awaiting rescue? Rescue she hadn't been able to give him. She tried her radio one more time, desperate for the sound of another human voice, but there was only that music.

Sophie waited for something to try the door from the

other side, but all was silent inside the tube.

Then a massive thrumming spread itself throughout the ship, and she clutched harder to the door. Her stomach dipped, there was a flip of vertigo, and she realized they were diving.

"Oh, God," she moaned, thinking of the millions of gallons of black, storm-tossed ocean that now pressed down upon her. What was the dive depth of a sub this old? Did it matter? It was far too deep for her to make her way to the surface without gear – she would be cut off from any possible chance of reprieve. Panic made her breath come fast and shallow, even as her survival instinct fought to gain control. There was a way out of this for her. There had to be.

Then a new sound reached her ears. The drag and scrape of thick scales against metal, coming from the tube behind her. She went still, desperate to be wrong, but something touched her in the darkness.

Before the rows of curved teeth closed on her calf, before she felt herself being pulled into a squeezing gullet and eaten alive by the ghost of something that could not be, Sophie knew that all her years of terror at the unknown denizens of the deep had been justified. There was no triumph in the discovery, and she began to scream.

PROJECT WHALE SONG

BY KAY HANIFEN

Incident Report:

Attached is a transcript of audio recovered from the Black Box of the USS Thurston *at Point Nemo along with my supplemental notes:*

"Mayday. Mayday. I am Doctor Lindsay Abara of the United States Scientific Vessel Thurston. I am the lone survivor of some kind of sonic attack that left the rest of the crew dead and I require immediate assistance. I repeat, I am the lone survivor of my crew and require immediate assistance. Please respond.

"Mayday. Mayday. I'm alone and stranded at sea.

There's something below the boat. I think it's what killed the crew. It's massive. I've seen blue whales, and whatever this is would eat them as a snack. There are some protrusions out of the water a quarter kilometre in each direction. If I didn't know better, I'd call them islands. But I'm at Point Nemo. The closest human life is on the international space station and the closest landmass is more than a thousand miles away. Landmasses don't just appear, and they definitely don't move. What is that? A head? A tail? It's grey and iridescent like an oil slick in the afternoon sun. I'm trying to make out the shape of these protrusions but staring at them for too long makes me nauseous. I can't comprehend the size of this thing. How does something so massive survive in a place with so few nutrients?

"I see the protrusions sinking back under the water. If you can hear me, please send help.

"Mayday. Mayday. Can anybody hear me? I'm stranded and alone. Please send help.

"Mayday. Mayday.

"Mayday. Mayday. I don't know why I'm bothering. Who's gonna hear it? Aside from the thing below the boat, there's nothing else here. No fish. No birds. Nothing but flat water as far as I can see. The good news is that I have plenty of provisions. We were halfway into our research trip here, and we packed enough canned food and non-perishables to feed our crew of thirteen. Now it's just me and all this food. The bad news is everything else.

"I don't know if anyone can hear me, but when we don't return, someone will come looking. Hopefully, I'll be alive and able to tell my story, but if not, the black box should record it so we don't become another mystery for true crime enthusiasts and conspiracy theorists. My name, as I said, is Doctor Lindsay Abara. I was born in America to Nigerian parents who emigrated to teach physics. When I was young, a case of meningitis left me deaf. In learning to manage it and trying to gain some of my hearing back though medical procedures like my cochlear implant, I became fascinated with the science of sound. It became the focus of my major, and I wrote my doctoral thesis on sonar mapping. When I heard about Project Whale Song, I knew I had to be a part of it.

"I know it's supposed to be classified, but screw it. I'll probably be dead by the time you find this anyway.

"Project Whale Song is experimental sonar mapping technology. Generally, low frequency sounds are used for long range, while higher frequencies are for detailed shorter ranged images. This new technology, though, used a frequency that would give us long-ranged, *detailed* sonar mapping. Naturally, the Navy loved this idea, and funded the inventor—Dr. Michael Williams'—expedition to test it out in the field. Dr. Williams chose Point Nemo because he wasn't sure how sea life would react, and this was the closest thing to a controlled environment we could get in the ocean—and, since no one goes here, we don't know much about it. Obviously. In our defence, who could have predicted a sea monster?

"I'm not sure how I felt about Dr. Williams. He mostly kept to himself, only leaving his cabin when we were testing the device. He'd mutter, grumble, adjust the frequencies, and then disappear. Once I caught a glimpse of his notebook, but it made no sense. It was all in code or a language I didn't recognize.

"I liked his PhD student, though, Maria Lewis. She was short, spunky, and we got into serious debates about silly things like whether Greedo or Han shot first. She was also brilliant, and would have had a bright future ahead of her.

"And then there was Dr. Aaron Smyth. He, like, Michael Williams, was a bit odd, but far less reclusive. He reminded me of those boys who knock on my door to ask me if I've heard about my Lord and Saviour, Jesus Christ. He was just too clean cut, too cheery, his smile too wide and too white. But he had an edge to him, the gleam of a fanatic in his eye.

"The rest of the crew were Navy sailors who kept the ship up and running. I only met Captain Ellis once. He shook the hand of every member of the crew and told us not to bother him unless there was an emergency.

"It was lonely, being the only deaf black woman on the ship. Maria and I could commiserate about all the testosterone, but I still felt as though I was in my own Point Nemo among the crew.

"For a week, we went about our business without much happening. The technology seemed to be working as intended, even if Smyth and Williams seemed unsatisfied for some reason. From my perspective, it was all working exactly as intended.

"But then the seismic activity started. It was Maria who noticed first. Small earthquakes along the seabed. I knew we were near a tectonic plate, so I didn't think much of it at first, and didn't start worrying until the ship violently pitched and yawed one morning. I'd never seen Smyth and Williams so excited. In that moment, I realized that Maria and I had been lied to. Whatever this experiment was, it had nothing to do with sonar mapping.

"The other two doctors began to shut us out. Literally. They kept the room with our equipment locked and held onto the keys. I know that academia has a racism and sexism problem, but that was just absurd, bordering on childish. I cornered Williams about it.

"'What are you doing in there?' I asked.

"'That's none of your business,' he said. He had bags under his eyes as though he hadn't slept since the boat began to regularly experience the effect of the seismic activity. Honestly, I hadn't slept much either.

"'The Hell it isn't,' I said, 'I'm as much a part of this team as anyone else.'

"'You have no idea what you're talking about,' he said, pushing past me and into his room.

That night, at dinner, Maria seemed distracted. When I asked what was wrong, she snapped back to awareness. 'Sorry, I—Do you hear that?'

"'Hear what?' I asked.

"'It's like this… humming. Like if a beehive could play a melody. You really don't hear it?'

"I shook my head and tapped my implants. 'Probably something these babies can't pick up.'

"She blinked, seeming to shake the fog away. 'Right, sorry. It's…it makes me feel strange, like the buzzing is reverberating within me and out of me.'

"'You hear it too?' Smyth asked, appearing as though from nowhere. 'Isn't it beautiful?'

"'I don't like it," she said in a small voice, like that of a child refusing to eat their vegetables.

"'It's the music of the spheres,' Smyth continued as though he hadn't heard her. 'The world is so loud nowadays. You have to travel someplace quiet to truly hear the cosmic reverberations of *musica universalis*.'

"I hadn't quite known what to make of Smyth until that moment, but I saw that fanatic's gleam in his eye, and I knew that whatever they were working on was a lot more dangerous than I thought.

"That night, I was awoken by a lurch of the ship so violent that it sent me sprawling out of my bed. I leapt to my feet, forgetting to put my hearing aids in as I ran out to see what was going on.

"The deck of the ship was pure chaos. Sailors were screaming in silence, bashing their heads against the wall, the ground. I saw one take a screwdriver, press it to his ear, and… let's just say I was no longer the only hard of hearing person on the ship. I tore my eyes away only for them to be drawn to the tempestuous water. It bubbled as though it was boiling, tentacles shooting out at random intervals.

"Smyth, Williams, and Captain Ellis stood at the ship's bow arguing about something. I couldn't read their lips at this distance and especially not in the dark. The two doctors were holding up a bound and gagged Maria. God, were they going to *sacrifice* her?

"Then, all at once, everything froze. Whatever sound had sent the sailors to extremes to unhear it had stopped. And a great eye emerged from the water.

"The eyes of a Colossal Squid are the largest of any known series. They're about the size of a soccer ball. This… thing's eye was almost as large as the ship.

"They held up Maria as though she was Andromeda about to be sacrificed to the Kraken. But this Kraken was not appeased. It let out a shriek that I felt reverberate to my bones, rather than be heard.

"When I woke, my nose and ears were tacky with blood and everyone was dead. My hearing aids still work… barely. They aren't great, but still better than nothing if anyone finds me. If you're listening, I'm still here. I've been rationing the food and fuel and estimate I can last at least another month, maybe two. Please. Come find me… even if it's just my corpse.

"If anyone's out there, I want you to know that I've been piecing together what happened. It was something that Smyth said: the music of the spheres. I think that whatever they were doing with the sonar woke the creature below. I've been comparing the sound they were producing to the ambient noise that the earth emits to the frequency of our sonar mapping technology. They're inverses of each other. If the thing below picked this spot to hibernate, it was probably because, in this loud world, this is the quietest spot it could find. And then we come in, playing the sound of nails on a chalkboard. I'd be angry too. The one thing I don't understand is *why*. Smyth seemed to worship it, and Williams wanted to study it, but where does the military fit into this? Did they want to use the creature as some kind of weapon? Ha. Good luck with that.

"The creature has been moving below me; whether it's to finally sink me or go back to bed, I don't know. And that's the worst part. I almost wish my death was as quick as those of the rest of the crew, but no: either it sinks me, or I starve. I haven't tried turning on the engine for fear that it would lash out. I never expected death to be so boring, between the horror of being stranded in the most isolated place on earth with an unfathomably huge sea monster below me. Please find me. I don't want to die alone.

"I'm sorry, Mama. I'm sorry, Baba, I love you both.

"Something is irritating the creature. It's been thrashing and the Thurston is taking on water. I think this will be my last transmission."

Additional Notes:

The wreck of the Thurston *was recovered approximately two days after the final transmission. We have reason to believe that the sounds of the rescue ship had enraged the creature, causing it to sink the boat and take the life of Dr. Abara. Unfortunate.*

As for Captain Ellis, it appears he believed that the creature was the Biblical leviathan and convinced the Navy to fund the project in the hopes of unleashing it and ushering in the apocalypse. Considering that we're all still here, it's obvious how well that plan worked. There has been no sign of the creature since the boat sank. Probably for the best it went back to sleep. No further action is needed.

THE ANGLER AND THE RAVEN

BY JOSHUA MARSELLA

Fisherman's Island, Chesapeake Bay
1856

Rolling, white-capped waves crashed into the sandy shore as a raven fussed over some obscure object protruding from the sand. A man nearby woke from his restless slumber. The morning sun had yet to rise; still, the man opened his eyes and stretched upon his bed roll, letting out a ferocious, guttural groan that spooked the raven from its inquisition. The flashing eye of the Cape Henry lighthouse drew his attention towards the Chesapeake.

Jeremiah Hornsbury had set up camp on the south side of Fisherman's Island with the intent of resting only a day before heading back up the interior coast of the peninsula. Since leaving his quartermaster position on the cargo ship *Friend of the Seas* following a tragic accident, he preferred to work in solitude.

Speckled trout and mackerel provided his meagre living, paddling his rickety skiff along the shoreline and selling his catch to the ships at the nearest marina. Chesapeake Bay was a thriving waterway, so this was lucrative business even for a lone angler.

Jeremiah dressed himself, checked his belongings, then poked at the few remaining embers from the previous night. With a fistful of dry driftwood and blades of dune grass, he rekindled the fire, kneeling beside it to warm his chilled bones.

His thoughts returned to the raven. The bird was the first living creature he'd seen inhabiting the island. Spotting a scavenger on the ghost-like isle surprised Jeremiah, considering the lack of sustenance it provided.

As the fire found life, it forced outward the darkness of the surrounding shore. The flickering light exposed the peculiar object at which the raven had been curiously pecking.

He placed another slab of driftwood on the blaze before approaching the object. Cold sand between his toes and the sea breeze chilled his flesh as he left the comforting campfire.

Inching his way closer to the object, he heard what

sounded like a soft whimper floating along the breeze. He paused to look around, expecting to find the raven perched nearby. The immersed stern of the skiff creaked and moaned against the pressure of the rising tide. Not entirely convinced that this was the noise's source, he waited and listened for the sound again. Hugging his arms against his chest for warmth, he released a cloud of breath then pressed on.

Settling onto his knees, the wet sand dampened his trousers as he inspected the object with the little light he had at his disposal. What he could see sticking out of the sand was round like a stone, textured like the bark of a tree, with a colour as dark as ebony.

Jeremiah reached down to feel the object but pulled back his hand.

Not just yet, he thought. *I'll dig around it first.*

Looking around the surface of the sand, he eyed a piece of driftwood within reach, and with it began to dig around the object. His labour was fleeting as the object was quite small—no larger than a coconut. Having decided that his curiosity was far more predominant than any unforeseen danger, he carefully cupped the object between his numbed hands and walked it back to the fire for closer examination.

The heat was a blessing on his skin. He knelt back down beside the campfire and inspected the object. Covered in a layer of wet sand, he gave it one good tap against his open palm. The sand cascaded onto the ground, revealing two sets of symmetrical holes.

Jeremiah recognized it as the skull of a child almost immediately. Although he was unnerved, he did not let it go. Instead, he gazed deeply into the dark, empty eye sockets as though lost in a painful recurring memory of the past.

A tear rolled down his cheek.

The sound of the crashing tide stole his attention, and he stared as the Cape Henry made a pass over the empty bay.

Looking down at the skull, he saw that the light of the fire shone through the left eye socket. With furrowed brows, he rotated the skull and saw a jagged, acorn-sized opening.

Somewhere nearby, a childlike giggle floated by on the wind, sweeping through the blades of dune grass. This time, he was certain it was not the skiff.

“Hello?” Jeremiah called. “Who goes there?”

He looked around as far as the light would reach but saw no movement beyond the swaying grass.

The sky was a deep shade of indigo, giving off the slightest hint of a not-too-distant sunrise beneath a band of golden horizon. The water reflected an infinite space carrying ripples of shadow that appeared then disappeared amongst the rising tide.

Following the brief appraisal, Jeremiah spared a few moments to bury the skull in the sand before reciting two prayers. One for eternal rest and one for salvation.

Having no intention of returning to this inhospitable beach, he gathered up his belongings, packed them into the hull of the skiff, then returned to douse the fire.

A thick pillar of smoke rose up as he relieved himself onto the orange embers. A stiff breeze pulled the steam downward and he peered out over the water. The distant beam of the Cape Henry silhouetted the shape of a ship on the horizon. A pillow of thick smoke enwreathed the hull of the ghostly vessel as though she were ablaze.

He tugged up his collar, cutting short the shiver running down his neck. The bay was active all hours of the day, but the angler felt that there was something eerily familiar about the ship.

Jeremiah pulled up his trousers then returned to the skiff to push off into the water. After all, 'early worm gets the bird' *was* his motto.

Grabbing hold of the skiff, his toes dug into the sand as he thrust the vessel onto the water before climbing on board.

Looking back out to the horizon, he paused. To his surprise, the passing ship was nowhere in sight. The fog was rapidly extending its presence across the bay, bringing with it a malodorous stench redolent of burning timber… and something else.

Curious, he thought.

Back on shore, the raven got to work, pecking into the ground where the blackened skull had been buried. Beneath its beak, the sand began to radiate and pulse with a fiery, crimson glow, sending threads of smoke up into the bird's lifeless eyes.

With an exasperated *caw*, the raven flew off over the island, leaving the grave and its own curiosity behind.

—

Jeremiah paddled his way out onto the bay. Beads of cold sweat slid down his temple from the exertion. Steam, rising off his neck and head, evaporated amongst the cold air of the dawn.

Against his better judgement, he directed the skiff out into the fog where the deep, dark waters hid his desired catch. The creaking hull was a welcome solace from the eerie silence brought on by the seemingly thickening fog.

Unable to see beyond the sides of the hull, he reached down, pulled up the anchor, and set it down between his feet. Feeling around under the bench, his fingers found the anchor line. Pulling on it, he laid the rope across his lap. Finally, he swung the anchor out over the bow and with a splash, lowered it into the murky depths below.

Slowly, he fed the anchor line through his hands, awaiting the sudden *thud* of the bottom. Feeling a tug on the rope, he gripped it to halt the anchor's descent.

His imagination conjured up the nightmarish image of a giant cephalopod wrapping its enormous tentacles around the anchor before finding its way to the hull of the skiff and tearing it to pieces.

He shook loose of the dreadful thought and chuckled at himself. Perhaps he'd missed his calling as a fiction novelist.

Then, once more, he felt something repeatedly pulling on the anchor. It felt as if someone (or several someones) were ascending the line. He wrapped the rope around his hand and held on tight. A stubborn man, he ignored his nagging instinct to cut the anchor free and paddle back to shore.

Then, after minutes of struggle, all was quiet.

A moment had gone by without any more resistance, so he carefully leaned over to look into the pitch black water. With his hand, he swiped at the fog for a better view. All around the boat were pairs of small incandescent lights just beneath the surface of the water.

Eyes? He gasped.

Shifting his attention to the sky, he unconvincingly decided that it was only the stars' reflections on the water.

Still holding onto the anchor line, he sat back down on the bench. Just as he loosened his grip on the line again, whatever had a hold of the line started pulling it into the water with full force.

Jeremiah winced in pain as the fast-moving rope

seared through the flesh on his palms. He let go just in time as the end of the rope tied to the bow grew taut. The bow was pulled into the water a few inches, causing some to spill over into the hull.

"What in the devil was that?" he asked, frantically looking in all directions before turning his attention to the painful sores on his hands.

From somewhere in the fog, he heard the sound of a crying baby. Struck with fear, he sat still as a statue, hoping it would stop, but it kept on wailing. The crying regurgitated painful memories of the tragic accident that had led him to his current state of affairs.

"Please… shut up," he said on the verge of tears. "Please stop! I can't take it."

The sound seemed to be moving closer and grew louder as he begged for mercy.

He cupped his hands across his ears to block the sound but quickly pulled them away, reeling from the pain in his palms. Leaning over the side, he dipped his hands into the cold water, doing his best to ignore the cries surrounding the skiff. The coolness of the Chesapeake felt good on the rope burns. He let out an exasperated sigh of relief as the crying stopped.

Resting his chest on the side of the hull, he relaxed and let his hands soak. Closing his eyes, he began to worry about how he'd paddle back to shore, never mind do any fishing, with his mangled hands. Still, he welcomed the silent reprieve.

The air grew calm and the gentle breeze felt nice on his skin, damp with perspiration.

Suddenly, he was startled by what felt like a small hand grabbing hold of one of his fingers. Before he had time to react, the index finger of his other hand was bitten.

"Bastard!" He pulled back his arms, toppling backwards into the belly of the skiff. Landing on his fishing pole, it snapped in half, causing the line to slacken. In one swift motion, the hook dropped free from the line guide, tore through the fabric of his shirt, and buried itself deeply in the soft tissue of his armpit.

"Son of a whore!" He screamed, belly up in the skiff. He tried to sit up, but the fishing line was tangling on something, tearing at his flesh.

Lying back to relax the tension on the hook before making his next move, Jeremiah looked around and saw the fog beginning to dissipate around him. With his free arm, he felt around under him for the tackle box to retrieve his blade. The sharp prick of a loose hook in the meat of his index finger sent a surge of pain up his arm. He let out a scream as he yanked his hand back.

All around him, uproarious laughter erupted out of the fog, seemingly aimed directly at his misfortune. The eerie, heartless chortle of children who had no business being out on the water surrounding the skiff.

The wailing of a baby returned, an unwelcome contrast to the taunting laughter.

"Be quiet! Go away, you… demons. You… ghosts!"

That's it, he thought. That had to be it. There weren't *really* children out here on the Chesapeake. That'd be foolish. He was hearing the laughter of spirits.

But that's impossible! Ghosts aren't real, he thought, unconvincing even to himself.

"I said shut *up*, you monsters—"

He cut his command short as he spotted something slowly slithering up over the starboard lip of the boat just beyond his feet. In the darkness, it looked to be a set of tiny fingers. Trying to slide back further into the hull out of its reach, he stopped when the hook tore into his skin.

Another set of fingers appeared on the port side. Then another right beside his head. And another, behind him at the stern. Soon, there were tiny hands gripping all sides of the skiff and Jeremiah had nowhere to go. Like a fish in a net, he was trapped.

His heart thumped erratically inside his chest. Once more, he reached down into the hull searching for his knife. This time, he came across his gaff and held it out like a spear, ignoring the throbbing pain in his hand.

"Stay back! I'll kill you all!" he screamed, a trembling, desperate anger evident in his voice. "I'll gut you all like fish!"

On all sides, the small hands gripped tightly onto the skiff. Then one by one, rising up out of the water, the hands were joined by the heads of the children they belonged to. Their eyes glowed with a ghostly luminescence that Jeremiah recognized from beneath the water just moments before.

In the bleak light of the morning, Jeremiah could barely see the burnt, malformed faces of the intruders: pieces of missing flesh revealing charred skulls; singed hair. One child's tongue dangled loosely from its missing lower jaw.

That was when Jeremiah recognized the smell that had accompanied the burning timber from earlier when he'd spotted the ghostly ship in the distance. It was the noisome stench of burning flesh.

"It can't be… this must be some kind of nightmare," he spoke aloud to the children. "Please. I'm innocent. It was Captain Mortis. It… it was an accident."

The dead children spoke not a word. Instead, as though taking cues from the nod of the older child clinging to the bow, they all began to rip pieces of the hull loose.

"No! Please… don't do this," he cried.

Chunks of splintered wood snapped all around Jeremiah, who could provide little resistance to the mutiny. Raising the gaff, he swung it weakly at the dead children, who easily brushed it off like a fly.

As they ripped and tore with impressive supernatural strength, the sides of the skiff rapidly began to disappear. Cold water began seeping into the belly of the hull, soaking Jeremiah's trousers. Unabashedly, he welcomed the warmth of the urine escaping his bladder from fear of his oncoming demise.

Desperately thrusting the gaff forward, he punctured the eye socket of one of the children, who made no effort to remove it, instead laughing at the angler's meek defensive efforts.

The starboard side of the skiff began to dip downward into the water. Jeremiah was face-to-face with one of the dead children, who leaned in and licked the side of his cheek with a slimy, blistered tongue. Jeremiah released the contents of his gut onto his chest; the dead child mimicked the puking fisherman before descending back into the water.

As the skiff struggled to stay afloat, on the verge of sinking, the children halted their playful destruction and dipped back into the water.

Jeremiah dropped the gaff, wiped the sick from his chin, and let out a sigh of relief.

No more laughter or crying. He started to wrongfully consider the idea that he may survive this morning after all.

Cutting through the fog, a hovering light was heading straight toward him.

"A cargo ship!" he said to himself, voice weak from exhaustion. *I'm rescued!* he thought. "Hello! Oh thank the lord. I'm here! Please help me!"

There was no response as the hovering flame continued its approach. Jeremiah stopped his pleas for help, in awe of the vessel.

As the massive hull of the ship came into view, pushing away the fog, Jeremiah's heart sank in his chest. He gulped, nearly choking on his Adam's apple from the dryness in his throat.

The hull of the ship was burnt black as coal, damaged heavily, littered with apertures, and coated in barnacles and algae as though it had risen from the bottom of the bay.

Jeremiah recognized the ship immediately from his time as quartermaster on *Friend of the Seas*.

"No, no, no, no! This can't be happening! It was an *accident*!" His cries grew more anguished with each syllable. "I beg of you, please show me mercy."

The fog lifted around the light of the torch and its bearer. Jeremiah stared, attempting to catch a glimpse of the person he pleaded to, but was unable to see beyond the shadow.

Holding the torch out in front of her face, a woman in a gore-stained nurse's outfit glared down at the man in the sinking skiff. Unbothered by his cries, one of the dead children appeared at her side holding a bottle and staring down at the helpless angler.

Finally, Jeremiah could fully see the horror before him. The woman in the nurse's uniform leaned over the side of the damaged railing. Half of her head was missing and her skin was badly burnt.

"Oh God… please… please forgive me." As

Jeremiah began to recite his Hail Marys, the bottle hit the inside of the skiff, smashing and spraying bits of glass along with its contents all over Jeremiah and what remained of the hull. He caught a whiff of the strong-smelling alcohol.

"…Thy Kingdom come, thy will be done, on Earth—"

The nurse let go of the torch and watched as it plummeted through the darkness, landing on the sinking skiff. In an instant, the timber of the skiff caught fire along with Jeremiah. He let out an agonizing scream that would have likely been heard from all corners of the bay were it not the break of dawn.

The flames engulfed his entire body and in his destruction, he prayed for the skiff to sink below the water, for to drown would be far more fitting for an angler than burning to death. Jeremiah had no such luck.

By the grace of God, his skiff remained afloat as he was slowly burned alive.

The smell of burning timber and flesh filled the air, but no one was around to smell it.

———

As the bright morning sun peaked over the dune grass, the charred hull of an abandoned skiff drifted onto the beach. Rolling, white-capped waves crashed into the sandy shore as a raven fussed over another obscure object protruding from the sand.

Scraping at the sand around the edges of the object with its beak, it slowly revealed its treasure. A blackened skull with bits of hair and flesh still intact, a bit larger than a coconut. The raven let out a joyous caw as it plucked loose one meaty eyeball before disappearing into the grass.

Jeremiah watched one last sunrise before the rising tide buried what little remained of his body beneath the sands of Fisherman's Island.

DEEP PURPLE

BY THOMAS GLOOM

It had been over seventy-two hours since the cruise ship last appeared on radar. News agencies were all over it. Not to mention the countless families and friends of passengers and crew who'd taken to social media to begin calling on the cruise liner, and the US Coast Guard, to divulge the truth of what happened. A ship that size didn't simply disappear without a trace, especially in the waters right off the coast of Texas. It had been scheduled to dock and unload in Galveston a mere three hours before it vanished.

Though the outcry was deafening, and the manpower involved in the search was massive, it had taken three days to find any answers. Yet, nobody could truly take credit for it. Just as suddenly as the blip had disappeared off the radar, it had then reappeared.

“But why are they only sending three of us down?” Greg asked, testing his diving gear. “That’s a gigantic ship.”

“This is just a simple reconnaissance mission,” Raul said. “There are a lot of unknowns here. We don’t even know if people made it off of the vessel before it went under.”

“Ah,” Greg said. “So, they want us to be the first ones to encounter the dead bodies?”

“Comes with the territory, my man,” Raul said.

Hadley smirked, but in her usual fashion, didn’t say a word. She was an observer. She listened and watched. It’d served her well through the last decade of working within the male-dominated field. Over ninety per cent of the US Coast Guard employees were men, but that hadn’t stopped Hadley from rising through the ranks. Her work ethic and professionalism couldn’t be denied. Her two male counterparts continued their incessant droning as she put on her scuba equipment.

“I get it,” Greg said. “But that doesn’t mean I have to be happy about it.”

Raul laughed. “I know a lot of people that would kill for this job. Just pretend you’re Sherlock Holmes. We get to be the first people to enter a possible crime scene.”

“Crime scene?” Greg asked, tightening his diving cylinder harness.

"Anything's possible," Raul said. "Call it a hunch, but there are just too many strange inconsistencies for this to be nothing more than some accident or malfunction. Who knows if we actually find anything, but I've got a weird feeling."

"And your little 'Spidey-sense' moments are generally correct," Hadley said.

"Whoa!" Greg said. "She talks?"

"She talks," Hadley replied.

"I've worked with her for over three years now," Raul said. "She typically only speaks up when she's nervous."

"All right… enough," Greg said. "You're making *me* nervous."

"No need to worry, Rookie," Raul said with a wink. "Hadley and I are experts."

Greg rolled his eyes.

"Okay, enough dicking around," Raul said, suddenly serious. "We hit the water in ten. Let's finalize our roles."

The surface was choppy, but not the worst Raul and Hadley had ever dived in. Greg, on the other hand, was terrified. He thought he was hiding it well, but the other two were veterans who knew fear when they saw it. Raul chose to not call attention to it, believing that once

Greg got under the water, he'd focus. What the kid lacked in experience, he made up for with pure, unadulterated skill. He was a natural, and his trainer, who Raul had a lot of admiration for, believed in him.

The plan was to breach the ship at either the captain's overlook or the entertainment auditorium. Once inside, they'd split up and move toward the centre of the vessel. If, for whatever reason, they weren't able to meet up in the main promenade shopping centre, then they'd resurface in sixty minutes time. They weren't there to find *every* answer, but they'd be able to gather *some* clues.

The trio dove beneath the murky depths, going deeper than Greg had ever been. While Raul and Hadley had been further down in the past, it had actually been a couple of years. This area of the sea was darker than any of them were used to, and it was strangely devoid of aquatic life. During their descent, they passed no fish, sharks, or whales of any kind. It was disconcerting, but they had a job to do.

Far away from the sunken cruise ship, in a secret military bunker on land, Admiral Toby McIntosh was being briefed on some of the specifics and mystery behind the watery gravesite.

Including the Admiral, there were only three men in

the large, dimly lit room. Computer terminals and advanced technological equipment hummed in the background. The whole scene was surreal, and Admiral McIntosh felt as if he was in a big budget military thriller film.

One of the men, who'd simply given the name "Max," pushed his glasses up on his nose and spoke in a hushed, conspiratorial tone. "We've known about this location for over five decades. Massive ships, small boats, military aircraft, and even a few search-and-rescue parties have gone missing in the area. There is literally a magnetic force that pulls from the ocean floor, and it not only draws vessels of all kinds toward it, but it fucks with search, navigational, and mapping radars. It's the Texas Gulf Coast's version of the Bermuda Triangle."

"And why have I never been made aware of this?" Admiral McIntosh asked in his usual stern tone. "How is this the first I'm hearing of it?"

"This is top secret information, sir."

"I'm a goddamn Admiral! I report directly to the President of the United States, for fuck's sake."

"And not even he knows about it," Max said.

Silence overtook the room as Admiral McIntosh digested the seriousness of the matter before him. He was honestly having difficulty in accepting everything that was going on, but he was a professional; he wouldn't let on that he held doubts. Then, a thought fell on him like a ton of bricks.

"Are my officers in any danger?"

"Any dive has its associated risks," Max said, nonchalantly.

"You know goddamn well what I mean," Admiral McIntosh said, a firmness in his words. "Have I sent them down there to die?"

"The likelihood is high, Admiral," the third man finally spoke up. "But I'm going to request that you watch your tone, sir. I know that in your little world you're pretty hot stuff, but you're in our world now." The man stepped from the shadows, his face now reflecting the blue light from the numerous computer screens. He wore massive sunglasses, but a jagged scar along his face was long enough that it still crept a few inches out from under the dark lens. His lips pursed into a smile, but it was anything but friendly.

"Yes," Max said. "There are risks, Admiral. And they are great, but they'll be worth it if your officers can offer any insight into what exactly has taken place on that sunken ship."

Greg was nervous as fuck, but luckily his extensive training had given him the necessary skills to keep his breathing rate in check, regardless of how he might be feeling in his mind. He looked down at his dive watch.

It had only been about five minutes since he'd split from Raul and Hadley, yet it felt like much longer.

The hall he was currently swimming through was dark and eerie. Thankfully, the guest cabin doors on either side of him were closed, so he kept his flashlight facing straight ahead and moved forward without stopping.

The water was strange down here. It had a thickness to it, almost like oil. It swallowed up the beam from his light so that he could really only see about ten or fifteen feet in front of him. He could no longer avoid the fear that had been working to grab a hold of him since he'd split from his two companions. His heart rate began to rise, but he kept his breathing steady. This was not the time to crack up.

A light flicked on in one of the cabins ahead and he grabbed the handrail on the wall, stopping himself dead. Could it be a simple electronics malfunction? But even if that were the case, what type of lights in a cruise liner cabin would function underwater? And were those shadows coming from the lighted room? Was some sea creature swimming around in there? The questions swirled like a whirlpool in his mind.

Greg thought of the man who'd inspired him to join the US Coast Guard in the first place. His great-grandfather, Joe. He'd never met the man, as he'd died in World War II, but he'd managed to talk his father into letting him read the old soldier's diary. What would

Great-Grandpa Joe do in this circumstance?

Resolve got Greg swimming slowly toward the lighted cabin. He unhooked his dive knife from its scabbard, tightening his grip around the handle. The blade brought another layer of control to the situation. Mere inches from the door, he steeled himself for whatever he was about to find.

The brightness coming from the room was staggering, and as he turned the corner, Greg was momentarily blinded by the light. Blinking his eyes for focus, he could make out two blurry objects. Within seconds, his sight cleared, but he wasn't ready for the scene before him. A shock of confusion shot through his body with the power of an electric eel.

Two old people, a man and a woman, floated before him in the small cabin, but they weren't dead. Their eyes were open and showed recognition as Greg came into the room. They then, in unison, cocked their heads to the side and smiled. No air bubbles came from their partially opened mouths, which, as impossible as it seemed, meant that their lungs were already full of water. How the hell were they still alive?

Before Greg could decide what to do next, the two unknown horrors moved toward him, their eyes glowing purple before exploding outward. Retinas fully detached, the four round orbs slowly sunk toward the cabin floor, leaving behind hypnotizing holes of bright brilliance in their skulls. Greg was frozen to the spot, entranced by the unnatural light which beckoned to him like seductive sirens of the deep. The colour was the most beautiful thing he'd ever seen and its call to his very soul was impossible to ignore. If he could just touch it, he knew all his struggles and problems would melt away. He'd be whole.

A small voice from somewhere in the abyss of his mind whispered a warning. None of this made sense. Greg was in danger. But escape was now an impossibility. The old man grabbed one of Greg's wrists, and then the other. He pulled Greg close and the purple glow in his eye sockets went dark as slimy, black snake-like creatures pushed their way out of the dead man's head. They came forth slowly, at first, but soon poured out in a flood. The slithering things wrapped around Greg's body, as if preparing him for an Ancient Egyptian burial. The last thing he saw, before the little monsters completely covered his face, was the old lady's head coming apart like a split melon, giving birth to more of the writhing creatures. He opened his mouth to scream, spitting out the regulator mouthpiece. The cabin lighting winked out, but vision wasn't needed for him to feel the squirming things as they forced their bodies into his throat.

Raul swam through the massive dining room on his way

to the kitchens. The ship's main eating area was full of corpses. The crowded ocean liner had disappeared from radar around dinner time so the place had been chock full of people filling their bellies, not knowing it'd be the last meal they'd ever eat.

A deep rumbling emitted from below the ship. It grew to a fever pitch until bright bolts of purple electricity shot through the room like some unholy lightning storm. The powerful energy made Raul's entire body tingle, yet the feeling was more pleasure than pain. The dazzling spectacle converged in a twirling tornado in the centre of the eating area before exploding outward, and into the countless dead scattered about. Their limbs twitched and danced, then their eyelids opened to reveal what looked like glittering amethyst stones.

Overcome with a dizzying mixture of confusion, fear, and awe, Raul grabbed onto the handrails of the nearest steps and held himself in place, waiting for whatever happened next. The dead came to life, or at least something akin to it, and drifted toward the kitchens. They moved in from all over, like ants entering their hill, before forming a double-file line to enter through the windowed swinging doors. Two by two, they disappeared into the galley.

After the last duo passed through the doorway, the doors swung shut and were still. How could so many people fit in there? Could he really even call them *people*? He knew that nobody would ever believe what was unfolding before him, but his vision didn't lie. Raul quickly moved from his location, curious at what he might see through the small porthole windows. Once across the dining room, he slowed his approach. He peered into the kitchen and was shocked at what he saw. The people, corpses, undead… whatever they were, were gone. The only movement he saw was the swinging of a refrigerator door as it closed.

Against his better judgment, Raul made his way into the galley, flashlight switched on and shining out in front of him. Everything was quiet and still, but he felt drawn toward the refrigerator. Unsure of what he might find, his muscles tensed as he opened the appliance. He never could have prepared himself for what he saw. Inside of that refrigerator was a glowing portal. Some hidden compartment of knowledge unlocked within his brain and he instantly understood where it led to. Raul was being beckoned, and he would answer the call. He let the flashlight fall from his grasp and, with his other hand, reached up, pulling the breathing apparatus from his mouth. Slipping off his goggles, he smiled and stepped into the other dimension.

———

Hadley was as tough as they come. She'd been attacked by the undead of the ship, and upon thinking she'd escaped, was then chased by hordes of the black snake-like creatures that, unknown to her, had already killed Greg. After she managed to leave the sunken vessel, the slithering monsters converged on her from all sides in the open water. Taking one final look back, she kicked her legs as hard as she could toward the surface. Every few seconds her flippers would connect with the pursuers, but still she swam. Her life depended on making it to the boat and nothing would slow her down. Hadley's mind was made up, and she was stubborn that way.

Her muscles were on fire and her breathing was out of control. She gauged that she was about two-hundred feet from surfacing when the creatures overtook her, but instead of attacking her face, as she'd expected, they seemed strangely attracted to the oxygen tank on her back. They pecked at it and squirmed their slimy bodies all over it. Realising there was no time for debate, she allowed her instincts to take over her mental faculties. Hadley unhooked the straps and let them take what they so desperately wanted. She took a deep breath from the mouthpiece before it was jerked from her lips.

Still, she swam for the surface.

—

The earlier meeting had not sat well with Admiral McIntosh. Top secret clearance or not, who the hell did that Max guy—or the man with the scar—think they were to speak to him in that way? The phone call the admiral had then received upon leaving the underground bunker hadn't done much to brighten his spirits.

The captain on the other end of the call delivered good news and bad news. The bad news was that two of the divers hadn't made it out of the wreckage and were presumed dead. The good news was that the third investigator had escaped with her life, though she was in pretty rough shape. They were still gathering the details, but she'd been found floating face-up near their diving boat. Her oxygen tank was gone. Based on early tests, she was most likely suffering from a condition known as "wet lung".

Admiral McIntosh got on a helicopter and flew to the military hospital Hadley was being treated at. He wanted to thank her for her service, face-to-face.

—

Upon arriving at the hospital, Admiral McIntosh signed in at the front desk and headed to the elevators. Hadley was on the second floor in Room 217.

After the short ride, he stepped off the elevator and onto a dark hall. All the lights were out, except for one that flickered as if on its deathbed. Definitely strange, but it was pretty late at night. Maybe things were kept dim after midnight so the patients could get some sleep. He moved down the hall toward the room in which Hadley was recovering. The hard rubber of his shoes clicked and clacked against the recently waxed floor. The admiral loosened his collar as the darkness drew in close, threatening to suffocate him. Ten feet from Room 217, he came to a sudden halt. The floor was wet. In fact, he was standing in quite the sizable puddle.

"What the fuck," he said out loud.

The liquid was flowing from under the crack of one of the doors on the right side of the hall… Hadley's room. He ran forward, stopping as he peered in through the rectangular window.

Hadley was sitting up in her bed, staring at Admiral McIntosh. Her mouth was agape and a flood of water was gushing out of her like a fire hydrant. A purple glow emanated from her eyes, brightening the room around her as if it were full of black lightbulbs. Every few seconds, thin bursts of lightning shot from sockets. Each machine in the room was gushing smoke, fried by the alien energy.

Admiral McIntosh was scared out of his mind. His pants where soaking wet and it wasn't from the water on the floor. Still, he grabbed the door handle and twisted. Fear gripped him to the core, yet he was drawn to Hadley. He was a winged insect caught in the seductive pull of a bug zapper. The door now opened, he stepped in, unable to help himself.

Hadley's lips contorted into a smile, the water still spraying out from somewhere deep inside of her. All of a sudden, the glow ceased and her eyeballs began to bulge out of her skull. One after the other, they popped out, dangling onto her cheeks. Black, snake-like creatures squirmed free from her eyeless sockets, plopping into the gradually rising water on the floor. The slithering things crawled up Admiral McIntosh's legs, breaking his trance. He turned and reached for the door handle, but then purple electricity again shot from Hadley's body, engulfing him in heat. His heart exploded within his chest with enough force to shatter his sternum, splattering the wall with blood and bits of broken ribs. His limp body collapsed to the floor.

The water continued filling the room. When it rose near the ceiling, the pressure became too great for the door's rectangular window and it burst, filling the hall with slick and slimy creatures. They rode the deluge into other rooms and to other victims.

This was the farthest inland the little monsters had been, and it was only a matter of time before they made it out of the hospital and into the lakes, streams, and riverbeds that stretched across the state like veins. Venom made its way throughout the body by riding the bloodstream. This cosmic infection would follow a similar route until it reached deep into the heart of Texas.

MELANCHOLIC BLUE

BY MOCHA PENNINGTON

---

heard some… *commotion* last night. Is everything okay?"

Lalisa's heartbeat quickened. She could feel its chaotic rhythm pulsating against her ears. Jennie's tone hadn't been accusatory, nor had it been soaked in suspicion. Her words had been carefully selected and delivered with a practiced nonchalance, like timid feet dancing around words too brutal to speak.

Still, a cold sweat excreted from her pores, gathered at her hairline, and dampened her skin. She tried on a smile and hoped it fit.

"Everything is fine," she said, despite the persistent throb in her biceps from last night's struggle.

Was Jennie able to hear the lie in her voice, see its noxious fumes wafting from her words? If she were able to detect any deceit, she kept it to herself and shifted her focus past Lalisa to the seemingly endless ocean encompassing them.

Why Jennie insisted on having their breakfast on the stern on such a somber day was beyond her.

The ocean was the deepest shade of blue Lalisa had ever seen, a reflection of the morning sky that was a churning marble of grays and blacks: a swollen belly, pregnant with disaster.

Melancholic blue, Lalisa mentally named that particularly ominous shade. She hated how active the ocean was now, how agitated it seemed to be, as if it adapted the sky's gloomy mood and took out its aggressions on the yacht.

Lalisa thought of Saul's yacht to be more like a floating mansion than a boat. It was at least five times bigger than the entire apartment complex she lived in… and much nicer. It had seemed so immense when she had boarded it last week. It had loomed over her, its brawny body of solid steel emanating a sense of dominance, power and security.

It had been a fallacy, of course, a magic trick performed by a cruel magician.

The yacht was feeble, powerless amid this ceaseless creature of melancholic blue. All it took was one wave with enough fury and determination to topple over the yacht and cast it into the sable depths of this monster's belly.

And that was what the ocean wanted, wasn't it? It longed to claim the lives of the remaining passengers upon this fragile yacht. Lalisa could feel the Atlantic's hunger as it slammed itself against the yacht, forcing it to sway back and forth in a drunken dance. How long would it be before it grew tired of playing with its meal? How long would it be before she felt the Atlantic's cold, ubiquitous hands pulling her into its abyss? How long before—

Bodies don't float if you puncture the lungs.

The thought startled Lalisa, jolting her back into the here and now.

Jennie stared at her across the table through narrowed eyes, her ebony hair lashed about her face by the fierce, salt-scented wind. They both wore their dark hair in a similar long, layered style, but Jennie's was achieved by getting a silk press, Lalisa's by having three bundles of a Brazilian woman's hair sewn in.

"What did you say?" Jennie asked.

"I didn't say anything." Had she? Lalisa was pretty sure her thought hadn't been given a voice. "Maybe it was just the voices in your head?" she managed to tease. Its execution was botched, the dull blade of a guillotine.

Jennie gave her a pinched smile. It quickly softened at its edges and lost shape. "Are you *sure* everything's okay? I know things between you and Ricky have been less than perfect." She paused, her eyes combing the heavy, wrought-iron table, as though she could find the right words among the carafes of mimosas and cloches of bacon.

"Look," Jennie went on in a sigh, "last night, I thought I heard—"

"*¡Buenos días, mis amores!*"

Saul's booming voice tore them from their conversation. Something enigmatic and fleeting crossed Jennie's face. Was it annoyance, relief? Lalisa was unsure, but she was thankful for Saul's interruption, for panic's clawed, malformed hands had begun to dig their way up her chest.

"Where's my brother?" Saul then asked, his English heavily accented. Saul's eyes traveled from the empty spot at their table to Lalisa.

"He's still sleeping," she said. It was the first excuse that came to mind, and it was the wrong one, confirmed by the confusion deepening into Saul's face. Ricky was a morning person, painfully so. Even with an hour or two of sleep, he woke with a vigor that she had learned to despise, among countless other attributes of his. "We *may* have had a few more drinks after we boarded last night," she added in a shrug and a smile that she hoped came off as cheeky instead of panicked.

"He's never been a real drinker," Jennie said. It was a lie; both she and Lalisa knew it. For the better part of a year, Lalisa had confided in Jennie about Ricky's newfound love for the bottle. "Go and try to wake him up," she suggested.

Was there a hint of a challenge in her tone?

Lalisa's stomach rose, terror washing over her in a

thick, gelid mucus. As she stood, she felt as though her legs were rubber and she would soon collapse, shattering into a million jagged pieces, revealing her dark deed in the form a bubbling, tart-like entity.

"Good idea," Lalisa said. She knew her voice had a slight quiver to it. "Food and water are the perfect cure." *Though I don't think his condition* has *a cure*, she thought.

"Let him know he needs to take over as captain for a bit. This thing can't stay on autopilot forever, not with this storm rolling in." Saul told her.

"I don't think he'll mind," Lalisa said, "All he could talk about was sitting in the driver's seat since you've suggested taking the yacht to Puerto Rico to visit your parents."

At least that wasn't a lie.

Ricky's interest in boats stemmed from his childhood. Ricky and Saul's father owned a fishing company and would often take his two boys out on the boats. He loved to tell Lalisa about the adventures he'd had as a child, and the mythical creatures residing beneath the sea that he and Saul swore were real.

It was Saul, however, who'd become successful enough to buy a yacht. "I expanded the family business to America, and Saul got a yacht," Ricky had once said, his voice laced with arsenic.

Wasn't the mention of a trip by yacht to Puerto Rico a seed? Didn't that seed bloom into a dark fantasy, a dark fantasy that struggled to emerge from the land of make-believe and into the realm of possibilities?

Bodies don't float if you pun—

"I'll be right back," Lalisa said quickly, slashing the throat of that troublesome, mental voice. She hurried across the yacht's lacquered wooden floor, hating how the vessel's sway had become more aggressive, how the water thrusting against its steel body was now more threatening. She pictured those powerful splashes to be a collection of eager hands, all fighting to be the one to reach onto the yacht and snatch her up.

She felt better once she was inside. The fog of terror clouding her mind had thinned but was far from forgotten. Though the roaring din of the ocean was muffled, she could still feel its fury in the yacht's deep lurches.

Get it together, she coached herself between shuttering breaths. Saul and Jennie had appeared unfazed by the approaching storm. Perhaps it was nothing to fear. Perhaps her mind had conjured this fear of the storm as a way to distract her from what she had done.

I know things between you and Ricky have been less than perfect; she recalled Jennie's words. She was one of Lalisa's best friends and was well-acquainted with the five years' worth of stories depicting Ricky's slow metamorphosis into a rancorous monster, but she'd only been given the skeleton. What was left omitted was the meat, skin, and blood of a tragic love story that wasn't suitable for publication; it would better serve as kindling to feed a starved fire.

It had become difficult to think of a time where their relationship hadn't been corrupted by a plague of calamities, when her presence had brightened his mood instead of banishing it into a shroud of darkness, as if she were a black storm cloud snuffing out the sun. Had there ever really been a time when his eyes were not tainted by hostility?

She had watched that hostility grow opaque over time, turning his eyes into hard, cold orbs—*wandering* orbs that desired everyone else but her.

If there had ever been a time where his hands had touched her with love instead of hate, she couldn't remember. The years' worth of fond memories lay murdered and dismembered throughout her mind—a massacre that shed no blood.

As she made her way down the hall to the cabin she and Ricky shared, she used the wall to balance herself against the violent rocking of the boat. She was thankful the corridor had no windows. She didn't think she would be able to bear seeing those wrathful waves crash upon the glass like a furious knock, demanding to be let in.

From outside, thunder sang out a sonorous note, and then lightening bolted across the sky, slashing open the cloud's pregnant belly. Rain fell down like bullets, adding more fuel to the Atlantic's rage.

Lalisa found herself in front of her cabin's door, wondering why she bothered to make the effort. She knew only emptiness awaited on the other side. Nonetheless, she went to turn the doorknob, and was struck with a glaring realization:

She was no longer part of a marriage, was she?

Perhaps the wound was too fresh, the staticky haze of shock too condensed for the realisation to penetrate and thrive, but she felt nothing knowing that she was permanently separated from her husband.

She'd expected guilt to hover over her like a swarm of bees, ready to envelop her, attack her until guilt's poison pillaged her of breath. But guilt was yet to find and claim her.

Thunder belched a low, resounding tune, like the warning growl of a cornered beast. When lightning struck somewhere in an unseen distance, the lights in the corridor winked a few times then went out.

An impenetrable blackness seized the tight space.

Lalisa backed away from the door, a cold, unexplainable fear seeping into her bones. She suddenly felt claustrophobic, as if the walls were closing in on her.

You're being ridiculous, she told herself, pulling in shallow breaths. *You're freakin' yourself out. You have nothing to be scared of.*

She then realised she did.

There was a pressure in the air, one that spoke of a presence. She wasn't alone. The moment that realisation crystalised itself into a cruel reality, she felt eyes on her, watching, hidden behind a curtain of darkness. If she had a flashlight and trained it in her watcher's direction, would a familiar face glare back at her, eyes ablaze with rage?

Her heart hammered against her chest like a frantic moth caught in a light fixture.

Maybe it was her missing guilt that stared at her. Maybe her guilt had manifested itself into some wicked, physical being, and now it was ready to fully become her.

That's impossible, she thought. Even her mental voice trembled with uncertainty.

Something shifted in the air. Lalisa wasn't completely sure what that something was. With the storm and ocean clamouring from outside, she had *felt* that shift rather than *heard* it.

She stood still, too frightened to breathe, her nerves wound wire-tight; just one pluck would be her undoing. And then, that shift happened again, but this time, she knew what that shift was.

Movement.

Somewhere concealed in the dense blackness surrounding her, she was positive now that she wasn't alone. The sureness of a presence was unshakable.

Who's there? she wanted to ask, but her voice

refused to work. It sat dry and stubborn in her throat.

There was movement again, a heavy scrape upon the plush carpet of the corridor. Had it been a foot that made that sound, its owner dragging its dead weight along the floor, or was it something legless, its immense arms pulling its torso closer to her?

The sound had no location, she realised. It could have come further down the hall or right next to her for all she knew. The uncertainty sparked something primal and unhinged, flapping in the pit of her stomach, freeing her from terror's paralytic hold.

Something cold, dank and rough grazed the curve of her calf. It was a tender, teasing caress, a simple stroke to confirm she was not, indeed, alone.

Her sanity momentarily cracked. Blind panic ran rampant through her. She raced back up the corridor from where she'd come, daring not to look behind her even as the lights began to flicker back to life.

Terror slithered up her throat and penetrated the dry lump of her voice, readying it to explode from her mouth in a ceaseless shrill. She turned a corner and collided with a figure. Her scream burst from her mouth but was prematurely amputated by the sudden jerk of the yacht. She lost her balance and fell to the floor.

"Jesus-Fuckin'-Christ!" Jennie shouted breathlessly. "You scared the hell out of me."

Lalisa ignored her friend and tossed a frantic glance to her right. The shuddering lights steadied themselves and illuminated the corridor. Was she surprised that it was empty? Maybe it was guilt that distorted her mind, made her believe things that weren't real.

"What's gotten into you?" Jennie's question pulled her from her thoughts. She had been practicing for this very moment. She couldn't turn back now even if she wanted to. She used the fear-tinged adrenalin soaring through her to add depth to her performance.

"It's Ricky!" Lalisa said, climbing to her feet. "He's not in our room." This was true; the dull throb in her arms was proof of that.

Jennie tossed her eyes heavenward, annoyance etching into her face. "I know," she said, stilling Lalisa's heart, "he's in the control room with Saul."

Lalisa felt as though a fist had been sent to her gut, stealing the breath from her lungs. Her vision tunnelled; a spell of dizziness befell her. Surely, she had heard wrong. She must have.

"W-wh-what do you mean, he's with Saul?"

Jennie frowned, the concern in her dark eyes softening the crassness of her expression. "Are you all right?" she asked, placing her hands onto her shoulders.

No, she wanted to answer.

She recalled the spout of blood, arching into the air before warming her hands, staining them in victory. Liberation.

Bodies don't float if you puncture the lungs.

"Did you *see* him?" Lalisa asked. *How would he*

even look? She then wondered. She envisioned a wet, pallid body sitting at the captain's seat, its joints too stiff to be fluent, chunks of flesh gnawed away by what dwelled beneath the sea.

"Of course I saw him," she answered. Her words came out in a breathy laugh that was a mixture of amusement and worry. And then, as if an eraser had cleaned her of any trace of humour, she said, "We need to talk about last night."

Jennie took Lalisa by her hand and led her through soft-lighted corridors, adorned with crown mouldings and gold-framed paintings. They emerged through a pair of dense French doors and were in the living room.

It was an enormous space of gleaming hardwood flooring and sleek, modern furniture. The colour scheme of white, silver and gold had made her nervous when Saul had given her a tour, fearing the darkness churning in her head might somehow boil over and leave smouldering, black stains in her wake.

They sat on a white leather couch, and Jennie took Lalisa's hands in hers. They were the same age, but Jennie had always seemed more mature, maternal.

"How long has this been going on?" Jennie asked.

Lalisa didn't know how to answer because she didn't know what Jennie was referring to. The plot to kill Ricky? Not very long.

"The abuse," Jennie whispered, squeezing Lalisa's hands. "I heard the argument last night, and he *hit you*, didn't he?" Her eyes roamed Lalisa's face, searching for bruises that were not there. Jennie's conviction wavered only slightly.

A bellow of thunder drew their attention from each other to the window across the room. It was a wide, floor-to-ceiling window, the heavy drapes pulled back to allow the terror outside to be on full display.

It was difficult to differentiate the sky from the sea at first. Both were black, both articulated their fury in a series of chaotic undulations. Their anger bled into each other, becoming one voice, a mob that demanded bloodshed.

Lalisa felt the ship rise, lifted by the callous hand of the Atlantic. It was then tossed aside. A groundless, weightless sensation rose in Lalisa's stomach, and when the yacht landed with a loud, sinister splash, the furniture jumped, became disarrayed, throwing her and Jennie to the floor among fallen implements.

Jennie let out a string of harsh words that weren't able to find Lalisa's ears. Her attention was summoned by the window.

Just as she had in the corridor, she was overwhelmed by the prickling sense of being watched. A million tears of the Atlantic streaked the glass, making scrutiny near impossible, but she felt eyes glaring into her with razor-sharp precision.

When she began to submit to the thought that maybe high emotions played wicked games on the mind, her watcher made itself known.

Near the bottom of the window, hands pressed against the glass. They were all wrong, those hands. They were too wide, like a catcher's mitt. The fingers were slender, long and tapered, like a stiletto knife. Were they just as sharp? Was that *webbing* between those fingers?

"…to get to Saul and Ricky!" Jennie was saying, Ricky's name pulled her attention away from the window. She had momentarily forgotten that Ricky was somehow alive and aboard the yacht.

"Why," she began aloud, and then internally finished her question: *…is he not dead?*

"Because they'll know what to do," Jennie hissed, clambering to her feet. "I don't know if you noticed or not, but we're in the middle of a fuckin' storm." Impatiently, she swiped her hair from her face.

They navigated their way to the control room, stumbling along the way under the ship's rapid movement. Lalisa couldn't entirely commit to the idea that Ricky was here. The last she'd seen of him was his ungraceful descent into the inky ocean. She had hauled him off the ledge of the balcony outside their room and watched his body be devoured by the sea.

How is he here? Was last night some sort of fever dream, a dream so powerful that her mind believed it to be true? Had her mind also conjured those grotesque hands against the window, that threatening caress from the presence in the corridor?

Am I going crazy? she wondered.

Something dark flowered in her chest: a truth haunting the outskirts of denial.

"*¡La tormenta se hace fuerte!*" Saul's voice reached them from behind the control room's door. An unmistakeable note of panic sat heavy in his words.

"*Déjalo venir,*" A voice replied. There was no emotion within that voice. It was almost robotic, the lack of life chilling. The voice was unrecognizable until it wasn't.

The same glossy hardwood flooring from the living room made up the control room too. Two plush leather chairs sat before a long panel of screens and buttons. Saul sat in one of those chairs. He swerved around with haste when the two entered. He tried to mask his fear with a smile, but his smile was flimsy, transparent, a band aid covering a fresh bullet wound.

Lalisa turned from Saul to Ricky, who stood at one of the several windows in the room with his back to her. He didn't even bother to toss a curious glance in her direction. It was eerie how he was able to stand completely still, unflinching, statue like. He wasn't dressed in the jeans and polo she had last seen him in as he plummeted from their balcony.

He paired a black, form-fitting elastane shirt that he worked out in with khakis. On one foot, he wore a sneaker; on the other he wore a dress shoe. Both were on the wrong foot. The outfit was unlike his usual dapper way of dressing. Lalisa thought that he may have intended the getup to be a way of joking, but Ricky Santiago was far too vain to joke about his appearance.

"How dangerous is it to be out here right now?" Jennie asked, nearly throwing herself into Saul's lap.

"This yacht was built to withstand a lot," Saul replied.

Lalisa seemed to be the only one who noticed Saul didn't answer her question.

"I feel like we were nearly knocked over," Jennie said.

Saul adjusted Jennie on his lap and pointed to a screen on the control panel. "The storm is strong," he said. The blue on the screen mocked the ocean and at the centre of the water was a swirl of a gradient of colours. The closer to the heart of that swirl, the angrier and darker the colours got. A patch of black was at the centre of the swirl.

Saul moved his finger to a blinking icon of a boat. "I'm trying to get us as far from the storm as I can." Lalisa saw that they were already in the storm: not yet close to those dark, angry colours, but it wouldn't be long before they were.

"It's pretty useless," Ricky said, still facing the window. He spoke in that haunting, emotionless tone again, his voice like a vacuum, sucking out any hope the three had. Lalisa also noticed he spoke without his normal accent cloaking his words.

Saul cleared his voice, as if doing so, he could dispel the awkwardness thickening in the room. "Don't listen to my brother, *Funshine Bear*," he said with a smirk, "I know I can do this."

Lalisa didn't think he could, but didn't want to say so.

She didn't feel safe. Not being caught in a storm, and not sharing this small space with Ricky. She knew she had killed him. She remembered the difficulty she'd had shoving that knife through his chest and into his lungs, puncturing them, making sure his body never resurfaced.

An effort lost in vain, it turns out, she thought.

Ricky must have felt her eyes on him because he turned to her. The movement was mechanical and stiff, his entire upper body twisted in a singular motion, like a cheap action figure with limited articulation. Was it fear that slithered up the length of her spine, seeped into her head and squeezed her brain, or was it something ambiguous? Trepidation? Foreboding? She couldn't say.

Ricky's features were arranged handsomely upon his face, but something was amiss. Self-importance didn't animate a mouth that housed a glib tongue. Cruelty didn't reflect in eyes that could cut one open, spilling out their insides with a single glance. His face was completely vacuous, a wax figure made by a skilful yet emotionally vacant artist.

"Let me comfort you," he said. The corners of his mouth spasmed then pulled into a vague resemblance of a smile. His full lips peeled back, revealing the white teeth he took so much pride in. His mouth remained frozen in that horrid position long after those hollow words left his mouth.

He hasn't blinked once, she became aware of. *His chest isn't moving. Is he even* breathing*?*

Ricky's face was more like a veneer that had begun to lift and peel at its edges—a costume that no longer fit—and the discomfort was apparent. It was almost as if a second, malevolent face writhed just under the first, twisting and poking, trying to blend in.

"What are you?" The words left her mouth without her permission. But it was a thought that had been clinging to the shadows of her mind, stealthily working its way up to be vocalised. Whatever it was that donned Ricky's flesh, wasn't Ricky.

The knowledge became contagious.

Jennie and Saul stared at Ricky, *seeing* him and all his wrongness for the first time. Saul gasped, a shadow of terror cast over his face. He and Jennie jumped to their feet in a chaotic flurry of limbs.

"Selkie!" Saul hollered, jutting an accusatory finger at the thing that wore his brother's skin. "You're a selkie!"

A slow beeping began to sing from somewhere in the

room, its song accompanied by a flashing red light.

"What the hell is a selkie?" Lalisa asked.

Ricky stood unnaturally still, that horrible smile unfaltering.

"It's... umm... it's..." Frustration crossed Saul's face.

The beeping grew faster.

Saul sighed. "It's... it's hard for me to say in English. A... a soul-sucker? A body-snatcher?"

"That can't be good," Lalisa mumbled. She backed closer to the door, wishing Jennie would follow suit.

A throbbing red light swept the room. The beeping turned into a long, persistent shrill. The boat icon on the doppler radar screen entered those angry, dark colours.

As if being powered back on, Ricky's smile dropped, and he shifted his vacant eyes to the window. "They're coming," he said.

Jennie's scream rang louder than the doppler radar's shrilling alarm. It didn't take Lalisa long to see what had caused her so much anguish. In the distance, a monstrous wave was fast approaching. It reached high into the blackened sky like a decaying arm emerging from the grave. It was impossibly wide, like a wall of concrete. And the way it curved at its top reminded her of a snake's mouth, its jaw unhinged, stretched to its max, its fangs dripping with venom.

The Atlantic was finished playing with its meal, and it was very hungry.

"Go!" Saul yelled at Jennie, giving her a shove in Lalisa's direction. "Get out of here. Stay away from the windows."

"No!" Jennie cried, struggling in Lalisa's grip. "Not without you."

"I'll be right behind you," he said, fumbling with a compartment beneath the control panel. "I need to take care of this first," he added. He pulled out a silver pistol from the drawer and pointed it at Ricky.

How could Lalisa be terrified for her life but smile at the same time? She longed to see Ricky knocked off his feet by the bullet, his body tumbled to the floor, as though his bones had suddenly melted away. The tug of Jennie's hand lifted the desire to witness Ricky's second death from her.

"Come on," Jennie said.

Ricky was no more, and Lalisa took great pleasure in the fact. That... *selkie* now masqueraded in her husband's flesh. Its death would give her no satisfaction.

She and Jennie were outside the door for all but a moment before a gunshot rang in her ears, rattled her bones, stunning her motionless. A second of silence passed before it was broken by an explosion of glass.

Lights flickered, struggling for life.

And then the world fell apart.

Lalisa was flung off her feet; a sense of weightlessness rose in her stomach like confused butterflies.

She felt herself slam into something solid. Her body was unable to register the immensity of its pain, for she was quickly flung again and slammed into something else so hard, she left a Lalisa-sized dent at her egress.

An orchestra of mayhem played around her.

Furniture clattered, broke. Dishes shattered. Decorations fell. Was Jennie screaming from somewhere? Waves pounded against the yacht with a deafening fury; they broke in through windows, greedy hands demanding their prize. The yacht spoke of its dismay in a low, mournful groan as it was yanked down into the blackness by the merciless hands of the Atlantic.

Lalisa was rolling down a slope, a slope that became steeper and steeper until she was no longer rolling in a painful heap of limps but falling, ricocheting off… the floor? The ceiling? An intrusive surge of the Atlantic chased after her, taunting her with a triumphant roar.

She knew what was going to become of her. Once she landed, the Atlantic would crush her, invade her every orifice, become her.

Or would it?

The yacht, not so willing to succumb to defeat, fought its way to the ocean's surface, shot into the air and fell onto its belly with a resounding *smack*, tottering to keep its composure.

The torrent that had pursued Lalisa swept her away,

dragging her down the hall and washing her upon a mahogany staircase. A heartbeat later, Jennie emerged from the water in a coughing fit. Spotting Lalisa, she managed to help pull her up a few of the steps.

Exhausted, Jennie fell against the staircase's railing. "What the fuck is going on?" she breathed, not wanting an answer.

Every inch of Lalisa was sore and throbbing. She was like a stuffed toy constructed of patches; each patch was at a different stage of pain. She was a vessel of hurt. She fought through her body's aches and protests to sit herself upright and gaze down the long, shadowy corridor.

It was dark but not completely obscure. The torrent that had pursued her flooded the space, about five or six feet deep. The surface would have been placid had it not been for the constant jolting of the yacht, trying to hold its ground amid Mother Nature's wrath.

She searched the inky water's surface, looking for Saul or his lifeless body. Surely if he were able to make it out of the control room, the flood's current would have carried him to this very spot like it had done she and Jennie.

"I killed him," Lalisa said. She spoke just to speak, to distract her from a sense that was just as overbearing as it was foreign. "Last night. I killed Ricky. You *did* hear us arguing. It was over something stupid. It's *always* over something stupid. He accused me of flirting with one of the waiters at the restaurant we ate at before boarding the yacht."

Was her body trying to tell her something; was that why an icy nervousness snaked down her spine?

"Ricky found any excuse to deem me an unfit wife and punish me for it. I knew I was going to kill him at some point on this trip, I just didn't think last night would be *the night.* Last night, for the first time, *I* was the one who hit *him.* Right in the back of the head with a ceramic figurine I bought in Puerto Rico. Then I—"

Bodies don't float if you puncture the lungs.

"Finished him."

"I know," Jennie whispered, her voice almost carried away by the storm's anger. "Or at least I thought I did. I heard the argument, and you... *finishing* him. Why do you think I was so adamant about talking to you about last night? I wanted you to get your story straight. You can imagine my surprise when I saw him with Saul."

Your surprise? she wanted to say, but her attention was stolen. Something was bothering her, pestering her like an uncomfortable elbow pressed against her side with no intention of moving. She studied the corridor and the body of water that sloshed at its floor. Something was going to happen. Unease prickled along her skin, trepidation thickened in the air. A warning, voiceless and incorporeal, came over her, urging her to flee.

"Jennie," she began, gripping the staircase's rail to

help aid her to her feet.

If Jennie had turned to her, waiting for her to finish, or if she'd opened her mouth to reply, Lalisa would never know.

Something sprung from the water in a blur, pouncing on Jennie, pinning her down onto the stairs.

Lalisa gasped. She pushed herself away from Jennie and the thing that held her down, her damaged body crying out with a myriad of complaints. She found herself on the landing, pressed against the wall, unable to take her eyes away from Jennie and what lay atop her.

She recalled those large, webbed hands with the long, stiletto-like fingers from the window. Those fingers were now buried in Jennie's shoulders, securing her in place; ribbons of blood wept from the punctures. Its upper body was humanoid: arms, chest, neck, head, and its lower half was a long, thick fin, which swayed back and forth like a cat, hyper-focused on an object.

Its flesh consisted of scales. Millions upon millions of scales in various shades of grey. They appeared to be larger and thicker at its torso and fin, smaller and thinner along its arms, neck, and head. Its hands, however, were smooth and grey, the skin parchment-thin. Three deep slashes were on either side of its muscular torso. Gills, Lalisa realized. They opened and shut in perfect rhythm, making a sick, squelching noise as it drew in the water surrounding it.

It emanated an awful stench, like a thousand dead fish, baking in the sun.

Jennie had been squirming beneath that horrible creature, struggling to free herself from it to no avail. She now seemed docile, as if welcoming her grim fate.

"Get the fuck away from her!" Lalisa yelled, rather pointlessly.

The thing glanced up at her. Its face was smooth and transparent like its hands. Its eyes, protruding, black circles, ate up half its face; it had no nose, just an indifferent slit for a mouth, which drew back to emit a low hiss, displaying not razor-sharp teeth, but yellowed baleen.

She felt completely helpless as she watched that thing, that selkie, return its attention to Jennie.

It hovered its face over Jennie's, its mouth opening impossibly wide. As if following a silent command, Jennie too opened her mouth, her eyes unfocused and glazed over. A sucking sound ensued. It was an airy sound, almost like a vacuum. Something wispy and smoke-like was being extracted from Jennie's mouth and pulled into that of the selkie.

Lalisa watched, caught in terror's paralysing grip, as Jennie's skin took on a ghostly pallor. It tightened on her bones, grew drier and then desiccated. Her hair detached itself from her scalp in fistfuls; her eyes bulged from their sockets then burst in an audible *pop*. It didn't take long before Jennie was a withered husk of herself, an instant mummy.

The life it sucked from Jennie simultaneously transformed the Selkie. It shed itself from its scales. They fell along its body to reveal Jennie's caramel-coloured skin beneath. Dark hair sprouted from its head, legs freeing themselves from a fin that had grown thin and hard like the shell of a boiled shrimp.

Lalisa didn't stick around to see that horrible creature reach its final form. She darted up the staircase, taking the stairs three or four at a time, staggering under the yacht's frantic movement.

She was crawling up the stairs by the time she reached the top floor. Pain sat in her body like shards of glass, exhaustion clouded her mind, made her movements seem as though she were negating her way through a room full of cotton balls. Fear of becoming what Jennie, Ricky and probably Saul had become served as motivation to keep going, no matter how difficult and seemingly fruitless it was.

She pushed herself along the carpet of a darkened hall she had been in only once when Saul had given her a tour of the yacht on that first day. She allowed herself into the first door she came across and locked the door behind her, hoping it would be enough to keep her safe from the terrors on the opposite side.

She didn't hold her breath.

Lalisa couldn't recall what Saul had said the room was for on her tour. The makings of the room were laid out in heaps of destruction before her. She waded her way through the mess on heedful feet, yet heavy fatigue and the pain ripping through her caused her to be clumsy, forcing her to stumble along the way before gravity pulled her to the ground.

She kept her eyes closed and paid little attention to the broken objects among the floor poking into her skin. She felt herself surrender to sleep, despite a voice at the back of her mind urging her not to. That voice grew fainter and fainter until it was no more.

A pounding lifted the veil of sleep. She moaned groggily, wanting to reach out for that veil and cast it back over her. She needed only thirty more minutes of sleep, just thir—

Her eyes sprung open at the sound of wood cracking. She was clambering to her feet when the door pushed open. Three figures filed into the room and stood abreast, their expressions completely alien to her. She recognized them, but at the same time, did not.

Lalisa stood in a corner in the room with nowhere else to go.

"Oh, shit," she sighed. Defeated.

DEEPWATER SIREN

BY NICOLA KAPRON

The bottom of the sea was darker than the blackest night. As my little sub drove forward, all but weightless, the whole world narrowed down to the illuminated interior and the shafts of light that blazed ahead of me. Incredibly powerful spotlights burned into the dark, but even they couldn't make it far from the sub. I gripped the controls with sweaty hands and glanced between screens as I ventured deeper into the black.

Well. It was mostly black. But every few minutes or so, I'd spot a tiny flicker of light, there and then gone, like distant fireworks.

28,000 feet. 28,100 feet. 28,200 feet.

"You doing all right, Jack?" Hazel's voice crackled over the line from her location on the research ship bobbing thousands of feet overhead.

"I'm fine," I told her. "It's brighter than I thought it would be."

This was my first exploration into the Challenger Deep, the deepest crevice on earth, but I'd been down here before. I knew what to expect from the abyssal zone. The hadal zone couldn't be that much different. So what if I was plunging into an underwater trench instead of trundling about on the open seafloor? It was still the same ocean.

"Brighter?"

"Yeah. I'm picking up some tiny flashes outside the spotlight radius." Even as I spoke, there was another one in the corner of the main camera screen: a miniscule burst of light that twisted like a minnow. "Aren't you getting this topside? I'm not seeing things, am I?"

The silence stretched just long enough for me to get worried. Then Hazel spoke again, her frown audible. "No, no, it's in the footage we're getting, too. I just... didn't notice until you pointed it out."

"Weird."

"It's weird in general. That movement—if I didn't know better, I'd say it was a bioluminescent fish."

That couldn't be right. "I just dropped below 28,600 feet. There shouldn't be any fish down here." Even the hardiest of hadalpelagic fish could only venture so deep before the proteins in their cells broke down. I wasn't that far beyond the barrier—roughly 27,887.14 feet—but I was far enough. "Maybe it's a crustacean?"

"Jack, I know crustaceans. That movement is all fish."

I grinned and gunned the ship's engine. "Then this is a great opportunity to discover something new."

Technically, this whole expedition was a great opportunity to discover something new. The ocean was the last truly unknown place on this planet. All our centuries of sailing, diving, and research, and humans still knew less about the bottom of the sea than we did about the moon. This place was as close to unknowable as you could get, and I craved that sense of diving into the unknown like an addict craved his next hit.

That craving was what had brought me down here. As I turned the ship toward the most recent flash, I felt it stronger than ever: the urge to *know*.

"Be careful," Hazel cautioned. "You only have eight hours of oxygen."

"Don't worry. It won't take that long to catch a glimpse of this thing. I'll take a look and then start diving again right away."

As soon as the words were out of my mouth, the light winked out. I spun the sub in a slow circle while I kept an eye out. Soon enough, it flickered back into sight beneath me, circling to the left. I turned the floodlights toward it, but saw only seawater and microbes. Either the light was faster than I'd thought, or it was out of range.

Three more tries confirmed it. Whatever was causing the light, it was deeper than I expected. "Hazel, I'm going down again. Our glowing friend is waiting for me."

She sighed, but said nothing as I sent the sub deeper. The engineering team had really outdone themselves. I couldn't even feel the pressure change even though the water outside my door was more than enough to crush me. The darkness grew thicker, if possible. My eyes tried to convince me that there was movement out there in the black—something huge and terrible and predatory. I ignored it.

What threat was supposed to be out there, exactly? Sharks couldn't survive this deep. Giant squid couldn't survive this deep. Megalodon certainly couldn't be down here, even if any had somehow survived. The hadal zone had been named after Hades, the Greek god of the underworld, for a reason. The deeper you went, the more desolate the ocean became.

To human eyes, anyway. The creatures that made their home here seemed to do just fine. And I was doing fine, too, as I urged the engine higher. The flashes of light had begun to descend faster.

30,000 feet. 31,000 feet. 32,000 feet, and the flash of light abruptly dove straight down.

"Not getting away that easy," I murmured, straining to keep them in sight.

"Do you think it's a school of something?" Hazel asked. "That might explain the frequency of the flashes. Plenty of deep-sea species use bioluminescence for communication."

"They usually use red light, since it's harder to see in the deep. This thing's flashing white."

"It might not matter. The other organisms living this deep may not be able to perceive light. The hadal zone is—"

Hazel kept talking, but I found it difficult to focus. There was something else to listen to—a song playing in the background. Had someone turned on the radio while Hazel was trying to talk to me? I tried to ignore it, but the volume grew steadily louder until I found myself nodding to the beat. The vocalist was an amateur, but her range was amazing. She got to pitches I'd only heard in whale calls.

Finally, I'd had enough. "Do you hear something?"

"Like what?" she asked sharply. "Is something beeping?"

"No, I just—it sounds like someone's singing."

A brief pause. "Jack, I can't hear anything. Where's the noise coming from?"

"I don't know," I told her, just as the song grew stronger. With each passing second, the singer seemed to grow less tentative, more courageous. The rise and fall of this wordless tune was beautiful. It was also loud enough now that I could tell where the music originated.

The song was coming from below me, deep down in the dark.

"All right," Hazel said. "Keep me posted. We don't need you suffering from DCS."

"Don't joke about that," I groaned. "Barotrauma's no laughing matter." Though it probably wasn't the cause of this. Decompression sickness only set in when the human body experienced a rapid decrease in surrounding pressure. I was going down, so the pressure was only increasing. Besides, the sub was built to make sure the pressure of the depths never touched me.

For a moment, I thought about telling Hazel I knew where the song was coming from. But she'd never believe me. Worse, she might demand I bring the sub up right now, and then I'd never find the flashes or the singer. I'd tell her when I was on the way up.

35,000 feet. 36,000 feet. 37,000 feet.

Another flash. This time, I was close enough to make out its shape.

"Hazel," I breathed, "it's a tail."

"I can see that." She inhaled shakily over the line. "Jack, maybe you should go back up. You dove a lot faster than our dive plan called for."

The light winked out. I let out an audible moan of disappointment and pushed the thrusters as hard as they would go. "I'm almost there, Hazel."

38,000 feet. 39,000 feet. 40,000 feet.

"Jack, something's wrong. These readings can't be right. The Challenger Deep is supposed to be about 36,000 feet. You've overshot that by… Jack, stop diving!"

I urged the sub to move faster. Fast enough that the

vibrations from the engine almost reached me in my sheltered space. The light was ahead of me again. This time, it wasn't a tail—it was a long fall of silver hair, finer than anything I'd ever seen before.

"Jack, I'm ordering you!"

The song was building to a crescendo. I found myself humming along.

"If you don't stop right now, I'm taking control and sending you straight to the surface!"

I jerked the sub to a halt. Finally, I could see it—see her—in the harsh glow of my floodlights. She lay on her side, drifting above the seabed, a vast shape of creamy white skin and drifting locks. Bursts of brilliant white light ran up and down the length of her tail. Her arms and upper torso had no lights. They would be all but invisible in the dark.

She was like nothing I'd ever seen before. Nothing anyone had ever seen before. And yet the shape of her was familiar.

As I watched, the mermaid stirred, another flash of light running up her tail. With a flick of her fins, she propelled herself forward, coming to greet me. Hazel was still speaking, but the mermaid's song overpowered her.

What I had taken for hair was the tendrils of an anemone, rooted in the mermaid's scalp and along her back. Her tail was the broad, flat paddle of a snailfish, edges tattered with age and wear. I watched, spellbound, as she raised her face toward me. Each milky white eye was larger than the sub, the cavernous hollow of her cheeks and the space where her nose should be big enough for a grown man to stand in. Below that were a set of massive, distended jaws that resembled nothing so much as those of an anglerfish.

Hazel was screaming. Distantly, I wondered what she was so upset about. Anglerfish live in the midnight zone. Finding one all the way down here was an incredible discovery. Assuming the lovely lady before me was an anglerfish and not something completely new.

With her mouth open wide, I could see even more of her—the lack of a tongue, the pallor of her flesh, the long dark inside of her. It wasn't enough.

I wanted to see. I wanted to *know*. That was what had brought me down here in the first place.

Her jaws snapped shut.

ESCARGOT, EXCEPT IT'S YOU

BY NIKKI R. LEIGH

I married my current wife Natalia not out of love, but because she possessed access to something I needed.

I get it. That makes me a shitty person. She doesn't know any better, and I keep her happy, so I think I'm doing okay. Living slightly above the moral low-ground, maybe.

I remember when she asked me: she said, "Maura, you love me right?" and before I responded, I didn't think of her. Instead, I conjured up an imaginary plate, adorned with the salty morsel I craved. There it was, the missing link of the dish I'd tried to perfect my whole life, and I said, "Yes, I do." I loved the idea of that snail, even if I didn't love Natalia.

She was a fine woman. But what made her finer was

her career. Not her driven personality and strong work ethic, necessarily. I mean, those things are good, I guess. They got her to where she is. But really, it's what she does. Where she goes.

Like today, for example. Today, she goes where I've needed her to since the days before we even met.

Today, she goes to the bottom of the Japan Trench.

And I go with her.

I'd been following her research for years. Found an article on the web about her attempted journeys to reach the bottom of the ocean. Saw a picture of her in her thick rim glasses and tight ponytail, looking every bit the scientist she is. I didn't care that her deep brown eyes smiled at the edges, and that her mouth was a beautiful rose pink with perfect white teeth nestled within. I didn't care that she was independently wealthy, donated to charity, and happened to be smart as shit.

Those might have been the things that made her someone else's dream woman. But me? I cared about two things. She gay? Check there. I'd have a shot at getting her to fall in love with me. I scanned that article, read something about an ex-wife, and figured that was my money made.

But more importantly, Natalia checked that second box. *What* she does with that brain. *How* she spends that money. She's a deep-sea specialist, on the cutting edge of mapping the oceanic terrain. Spends her time with a team of engineers, all sorts of science-y stuff that's supposed to be able to allow her to travel in a submersible thousands of metres deep.

She's going to put that little ship to the test today. 8,000 meters, to the bottom of the Japan Trench. And there, when she grabs her sediment sample, I'm going to send every prayer I know to whatever God there is that she takes a handful of the fabled trench snail with it. And I'll pray a little more that I can sneak one away from her lab once it's there. And maybe one more that I don't completely fuck up preparing it for the dish I want to present at my restaurant that'll earn me my first Michelin star.

So here we are. She's in the submersible. I'm in her lab.

She's getting ready to go below surface. Her little team is out there on the docks with her, fluffing her up as she gets ready to do the unthinkable and go where nobody has before. Down into the deep. One of the deepest places in the world, actually, the Japan Trench.

No one really knows what to expect. Up until this point, people have only collected chemical samples from the flumes around the trench. Only have *suggestions* of what might be there. Supposedly, there's life. Nutrient-rich sediment that can support life. That's what science *suggests.*

But the stories… those are a whole different kind of suggestion. Fishermen, divers, folkloric tales… all of them say there *is* life down there. That on the bottom of the seafloor lie thousands of crawling, fist-sized, sacred snails. Their shells are made of igneous rock, formed by the magma that isn't much further below the trench. The deeper you go, the more delicious life is. I'm betting my own life that these snails are edible, and that they will make me a star chef.

This snail means the world to me. I just know that it's what I need to bring my restaurant cooking to the next level. To bring that bit of exoticism to the plate that no one else can achieve. That it's going to taste a dream served boiled, seasoned just right, looking beautiful with that shell of hardened magma glistening on the plate.

The chatter on the comms cuts through the thick syrupy sweetness of my dreams.

Lana, Natalia's best friend and lead engineer, speaks softly.

"Can't believe it's happening, boss."

Natalia's voice is clear as day despite the thick plexiglass and titanium surrounding her. "Just a quick looksee is all we're doing today. Nothing too sensational." She's humble. She *better* be doing more than just looking. I need her to be grabbing too.

"And taking samples, right?" I ask.

"Not today, Maura."

My heart drops with those three words. I… I've waited so long for this day. To get these snails.

She continues. "We won't be ready for retrieval for

another couple of months. We need to know what we're looking at before we know what to take."

I roll my eyes in the safety of the empty lab. How scientifically…quaint.

In this moment, I have decisions to make. My restaurant and career are currently languishing in the mundane. I've only recently grabbed the attention of some of the great chefs and critics and I won't be able to hold onto them for much longer. I've heard talk of iron-enriched, decadent vegetables from a farm out west, evidence of a ticking time bomb before people move onto the next culinary powerhouse. I need to get this dish—this dish that nobody in the world could replicate—out and I need it out now. Not enough time on Natalia's timeline. Months? I barely have weeks to make something happen in today's climate.

So, I make my first decision.

"Natalia? I'm getting some weird signals in the lab here."

She's silent.

"Uh, some weird beeping and red lights on the exo of your sub," I continue, attempting to make it sound important. "You might want to send the crew."

Natalia sighs. "Fine. Lana, Boyd, head on back."

"Roger, boss."

I find a wrench and it's hefty and cold in my hands.

After a few minutes, Boyd and Lana enter the lab, heading straight for the computer.

“I don’t hear anything,” Boyd says, his voice a rumble.

“The lights were just on the monitor, I swear it,” I say.

Lana and Boyd huddle around the computer, eyes squinting against the light of the screen.

Lana turns to me. “Maura, I’m not seeing the—”

The wrench in my hand answers, the dull thud of the metal against her skull overtaking the gasp that escapes her mouth as her head caves in. The blow to her temple sends her to her knees. Boyd swivels only to meet the clawed fingers of the wrench, this time from a backhand I send his way. The force is hard enough to get through his thick skull, splitting his head open in an arc of red.

He doesn’t move again. Lana sputters on the ground. I strike her again, pushing the sound of her crushed face from my mind, my thoughts singularly aimed at the thought of what the trench holds.

With the two crew members disposed of, I make my way to the bay. The hammering of my heart covers the soft plinking of the blood as it falls from the lips of the wrench to the metal hallway below.

I hear Natalia asking for responses in my earpiece. “What’s going on with the ship?” she asks, persistently. “Lana? Boyd?” and after a few beats, “Maura?”

“Just coming to help them run a diagnostic. I’ll see you in a second.”

And I do. Around the corner, floating in the docking

bay, is my wife, surrounded by the thick plexiglass dome of the submersible. It's a small craft, just large enough for a single person to move around, with a set of arms and storage on the underside. Cameras are mounted on the exterior, tiny lights blinking, ready to record history.

Can't let them record me.

"Hey, honey, can you power down for a minute? Something weird was going on and you should take a look at it inside."

She looks at me, love in her eyes, and I feel a twinge of guilt at her inevitable demise. She has big dreams, the brains to achieve them, but a heart that can't see through my bullshit. She's blind to being used. I tell myself it's not my fault, that she should have known I was no good.

Natalia steps out of the craft. She really is beautiful, fit and youthful, full of energy. I almost wish I had room in my own heart for her. But cooking—my passion—it really takes it all. I could either have the love of my life, or a life worth living.

"Maura, is everything okay?" Her innocent voice pulls at whatever feelings I have for her.

"Just fine, Natalia," I say, my voice barely a whisper as I wrap her in a hug. My eyes catch the sight of the name painted onto the sub. *Maura's Sub Sandwich.* I hate that pun. I hate that she named it after me.

She doesn't see the wrench as my arms curve around

her.

She won't get me what I need, so I have to get it myself. I make my last decision.

I turn her body, pull it close to mine. Lifting the wrench to her neck, I grab both sides and pull. The metal crushes her hyoid, and it isn't long before she suffocates.

I glance towards the sub, open and waiting for me to drive her to the bottom of the ocean.

I don't know how long I'll have until someone finds the bodies. I don't know how long I'll have down there. I push Natalia's body to the edge of the dock, roll it over the side and into the water. I want her to sink, to reach the bottom of the ocean eventually, so she can achieve her dreams of being at the bottom of the trench. I'm not a complete monster, you know.

I hop into the sub and close the hatch. A lot of buttons and levers, but it looks self-explanatory enough. The design is sleek, and I send a silent thank you to the dead engineers in the control room lab for making the craft as simple as possible to drive.

I take a breath, almost as if I'm dunking my head in a swimming pool, and flip the switch that powers the sub. It whirs to life and I exhale, hearing the energy thrum through the machine.

My instincts take over, and before I know it, I'm manoeuvring the sub below the surface, marvelling at how easy this really is. Maybe Natalia wasn't as smart as I gave her credit for. Or maybe I was just as good as her.

Down and down I go, attempting to follow the HUD to the Japan Trench. As far as I can tell, the coordinates and depth are plugged into the machine, making navigation smooth as butter. I cut through the blue of the ocean, leaving behind my worries and guilt in a gentle stream of bubbles. My path scribbles an etch-a-sketch into the water, memories of every metre I descend carved into the depths.

I wonder if anything will know to follow.

I descend for miles. For the first hundred metres, the life is plentiful. Fish, jellies, bigger fish, sharks, seaweed… nothing out of the norm. I didn't need them. I need what's deeper.

I dig in, watching the display tell me that I'm headed for treasure. Minutes that feel like hours in the quiet pass. It's been dark for a while now. Nothing but the lights of the ship, though they land on nothing, as far as I can tell. I no longer wonder when I'll see the trench. I realise now, here in the dark, that there isn't anything to see. No sign welcoming you to the black depths.

I am the trench. In it. Swallowed by her mouth, which stretches in every direction.

Here, alone, I wonder if the snails are worth it. This feeling of insignificance in the endless dark. The death. Will I die?

I chide myself for my recklessness. I realize I don't

know what the hell I'm doing. That I have literally just murdered my wife and her crew and commandeered a sub I've never piloted to find some possibly non-existent snails at the bottom of the ocean, which may or may not be edible and may or may not change my life forever so long as I get away with the crimes I've committed.

I begin to panic, the blackness around me screaming, slinging insults into my face. Every inch of obsidian water that passes my window tells me I'm a goddamn idiot.

But I'm a goddamn idiot with only a thousand metres before I reach the bottom. A goddamn idiot who hasn't yet exploded from the immense amount of pressure threatening to crush me and the sub. A goddamn idiot putting a helluva lot of faith in a self-guiding watercraft built outside the government domain, funded with private dollars and a whole barrel full of gumption.

Another ten minutes of miserable, silent thinking, and I arrive. I feel the sub slow, hover, extend its legs and settle into the sand—rock?—whatever makes up the floor. The cameras relay a feed to the HUD, the lights powering up at full force.

When the lights go up, my whole world changes.

The blackness that stretches for miles in every direction sees a spotlight it has never before experienced. In that moment, I finally grasp what I'd done. I've taken over one of the greatest deep-sea accomplishments for what… snails? Which, now that the light is on, I don't even see.

The dark void may have disappeared in the light, but the emptiness remains.

At the bottom of the trench, I am truly at my lowest of lows.

Unless… the sand ahead agitates. A small eruption of silt clouds the floor, and I find myself holding my breath again, not wanting to make sound.

A rock breaks the sand's top layer. It pushes up, rounded, jagged, as if the ocean floor is birthing land right before my eyes. Pushing towards the sky, wherever it is, to get up from the depths, such a strange concept to my brain—which just spent the better part of an hour descending into the black.

The rock, about a foot in diameter, breaches completely, followed by an electric green, gyrating mound of flesh, smooth as a marble.

I exhale, resisting the urge to scream.

It's a fucking snail. It's *the* snail.

Prayers, answered.

The snail stops, looks around and I wonder if it can sense the light, the way its home is exposed.

It must not notice, or care, as it moves forward. I contemplate sending the arms of the sub to grab it, but stop when I see the rising sand clouds from dozens of other spots in front of me. I glance at the back cameras and can see them all around me.

Hundreds of the most exotic snails on Earth, heading right for me.

I can't hold out any longer, seeing the wealth of the gods in front of me. I press a button, grab the joystick that controls the arms of the sub. *Just like the video games*, I think, extending the arms to menace over the closest snail. I grab it.

The arm retreats to the sub, placing it in the storage below. I try to discern how many I can take, filling the stomach of the ship one by one until the display tells me it's beyond capacity.

I feel a gnawing in my gut, wishing I could grab more, not knowing if I'll ever get this chance again.

I take another snail into the arms of the sub, determined to carry it out just like that on my way up. I manoeuvre the claw so I can see it right in front of the window of the ship. The snail, with its bulbous feelers and vibrant skin, appears to be staring back at me.

Ugly, beautiful, *perfect*.

I try to imagine it boiling in a pot, try to picture the seasonings I'll pepper onto its skin. Paint a divine portrait of its gloriously bright skin and shining, rocky shell on a plate. I visualise holding that plate, smiling in a picture, an article about my Michelin star award.

The snail stops wiggling in the claw of the ship. I wonder if I've killed it.

Before I can set it down to grab another, it opens a mouth I didn't even know it had.

The snail screams.

The sonic shout penetrates the thick walls of the sub. I raise my hands to try and halt the sound, a futile attempt, I realize, as my hands feel the wetness of blood trickling from my ears. The scream alerts the snails within the belly of the ship's storage. They start to yell in synchronicity with their brethren.

I feel like I'm vibrating out of my mind. My skin—God, my skin—it's vacillating wildly, blurred by the motion of its movement back and forth. It's flaying me alive.

My eyeballs feel like a mound of Jell-O, flicked by some kid who'd rather play with his food than eat it. I try to see through the constant movement, try to find the switch to start the ship back on its course to the surface. My fingers find the button. Taking all the damn energy I have to push it.

The screaming stops before I can press the button.

I breathe, thankful that the torturous noise has ceased. My body feels like it went twenty rounds with a steel pole, every inch buzzing.

I raise my eyes back out to the window. See that the snail has tucked into its shell.

The rumbling begins.

All around me the sand builds like a fog. It feels like the ground beneath the sub's legs is cracking and shifting, and I pray that an oceanic earthquake hasn't been triggered. Minutes of tremors and complete sand-filled blindness have me babbling commands at the controls. The sensors on the ship are going off, sending stabs of pain behind my eyes, still recovering from the sonic shrills of the snails.

I think of Natalia and her broken throat and I know that I deserve this hell.

When the dust settles, I wish for the ground to swallow me.

In front of the ship, in front of me, is a snail that defies nature. Towering over me, at least forty feet tall, it looms, silent. The boulder that is its shell feels impossibly large—like a moon I expect to begin orbiting.

Electric green—just like what I now realise to be the infantile sea snails I'm carrying in the stomach of my ship.

With one look into what I assume is its blobby, ill-defined face, I know I'm fucked.

My fingers stab the button to send the seacraft into ascension, thinking I can blink the hell out of here before that snail can punish me for stealing its children. Nothing happens, except more sirens and a flashing light indicating that the ship is too heavy to properly rise.

We won't be ready for retrieval for another couple of months. Natalia's words echo in the ocean deep.

Fuck this. These snails might have been worth the collateral damage of Natalia and her crew, but not my own. I move to release the sea snails I've captured. Leave them behind, for now.

I could always come back. I could always—

The giant snail shifts. It snorts from nostrils I cannot see—*do snails even snort?*—and a cavernous mouth opens in what I thought was its chest.

The hole is lined with teeth like stalactites.

"Take them back!" I yell, jamming my finger into the storage release over and over again.

Even as I feel the snails fall from the ship, I know it wants more. Not just its babies. Revenge. I interrupted its sleep. The peaceful whatever-the-fuck kind of life it had here at the bottom of the trench.

With the ship relieved of the precious cargo, I stab the flight button again. The sub begins to whirr, readying itself for ascent. I cry as I feel the arms and legs of the ship tuck back into the hull.

The ship hovers.

"Hurry up you sonuvabitch! Go!"

It doesn't care that I'm practically sobbing as the humongous snail opens its mouth wider. It moves. So. Damn. Slowly.

The monstrous snail's mouth turns to a snarl. It opens its mouth again, this time sucking in with all its might. A vortex appears before it, and my ship, even with its attempt at ascent, struggles against the current.

Everything is loud and crushing metal as I whirl through the chasm of the sea, ever closer to the snail.

Everything is pressure as the sub strikes the dangling teeth of the snail's mouth.

Everything is pain as the ship crumbles under the weight of the ocean.

I explode from the ship, broken, beaten bloody by anything and everything.

Light disappears as the sub is destroyed. In blackness again, this time, inside the mouth of the very creature I longed to retrieve. I'm pretty sure I'm dying fast.

I wonder if the snail would have been edible raw. I wonder if the snail would have preferred me to be cooked. My ship was a beautiful shell, I think.

WEREWOLVES AND TENTACLES

BY SPENCER HAMILTON

Atlantic Ocean
Somewhere along the Outer Continental Shelf
About one mile beneath sea level

Piercing howls echoed out of the darkness behind Anastasia, spurring her on.

Faster... faster!

Serrated claws shrieked for purchase against metal surfaces, pulling the heaving beast closer, closer. They sent sparks in their wake, briefly illuminating the pitch-black corridor like muzzle flashes. Anastasia got a brief glimpse of the thing behind her shoulder: coarse, black fur, rippling muscle, frothing snout lined with yellowed ivory canines—and two bulbous, full-moon orbs, penetrating the darkness and staring right back at her.

Jimmy.

She turned her back on the animal and put on a burst of desperate speed. Her heart outraced her boots as they clanked over riveted steel. This damn place was a labyrinth, but if she could just get to this level's communications room, she might be able to warn the others before it was too late.

Jimmy!

Still, no response. The thing chasing after her was mindless; Jimmy was gone. And it was all her fault.

But that didn't matter right now. Because just outside these walls, crawling along the ocean floor, was something far, far worse.

It had been two months since the Void Hunters had moved their headquarters to this underwater dump. As compensation for the Coney Island fiasco, the U.S. government, suddenly taking their shadow task force seriously, talked big about the bunker. A steel stronghold, impossible to find, hidden from the world at the bottom of the Atlantic. The rest of the team, still fresh from Gunther's betrayal and Doc's death and the big showdown at Coney Island, were excited—finally, the resources they needed in order to protect the earth from the Void and the unimaginable monsters trying to escape it. But Anastasia knew better. Russia, America, it didn't matter where you went, the government was never to be trusted. It was all just another empty promise, a warm meal luring the child into the witch's cottage only to be snatched away, or upon closer inspection crawling with maggots.

The deep-sea bunker was massive, the amount of resources and engineering required impressive, Anastasia had to admit. It had been built decades ago and abandoned not long after. Anastasia was surprised the ocean hadn't crumpled this place down to scrap metal by now. Twenty-five hundred pounds per square inch—that was the water pressure at this depth. The weight of her life had always threatened to crush her, but Anastasia felt she may have met her match down here in the trenches, where nothing survived.

Well, nothing but the Void...

Of all the places to be trapped with a werewolf, Anastasia thought.

Jimmy– or the thing he'd become—was so close now that she could feel his fetid breath on the nape of her neck. She'd conditioned her body in the fifteen years since Doc had found her and Mikael in that Russian orphanage, could run at a dead sprint for thirty minutes before getting winded. But still, she didn't like her odds in this race. The human body simply wasn't built to outpace the powerful hindlegs pumping like pistons behind her. Not to mention—

Bang—pop!

She couldn't see it in this darkness, but she could *feel* it, like pressure in her eardrums: a part of the metal corridor, where the wall met the ceiling, crimping inward like a crushed tin can. The tunnel shook all around her, as if from an earthquake. But it wasn't an earthquake. It was an impossible monster, brought into this world by Anastasia's own foolish actions.

The tunnel walls juddered as if straining against the rock of the canyon trench. She could almost feel whatever monstrous appendage was wrapping itself around the bunker, as if it were coiling around her own neck, tightening, squeezing—

She would stop it. She had to. Anastasia wasn't weak, wasn't the hunted.

She was a Void Hunter.

Two months since they'd settled into the new HQ, yet she was still a mess. Anastasia felt like an exposed nerve, threatened by everything around her, the protective tissue never growing back. The psychic link she and her twin brother, Mikael, had shared since birth, was severed. Two months since Coney Island, and several more since Mikael had been ripped away. Yet still she felt him, felt their connection: always here but forever gone, like a phantom limb.

It was because of this that she'd been avoiding the rest of the team since they'd all arrived here in the bunker. Sammi had insisted she pick a room on an upper level, close to the others. Anastasia acquiesced, but she wasn't sleeping much these days, so her room mostly sat empty while she explored these lower levels. They tunnelled deep into the slope of the continental shelf, built into a system of snaking, steep-walled submarine canyons. This bunker was so old, there was no surviving blueprint that anyone knew of, so these bottom levels were largely abandoned. Anastasia liked to stroll through them, let herself get lost in the maze, half cloaked in darkness, half lit by flickering, buzzing bulbs. She'd often pretend she was on a space station lightyears from this planet and all its suffering. The black, crushing waters just outside these walls was the empty void of space; the *drip-drip-drip* of ocean water was liquid ammonia from a leaky power system. It helped to clear her mind of it all, to quieten the voices in her head, to dim the flashes of painful memories. Of Mikael…

This morning was different, though. This morning she was bolted awake by a nightmare. Not hers. This wasn't unusual in the days when she'd shared a psychic connection with her brother—dreams, they'd found, were impossible to control, and they'd often subconsciously thrust their nightmares at each other, giving the other person a rude awakening like a charley horse or a nasty hangover. She'd thought all of that might have stopped after Mikael's death, but—lucky her—she was stuck with her brother's boyfriend, Jimmy. That British bastard. She hated him for bonding so strongly with Mikael, thus forcing this nascent connection. Jimmy had dreamed of Mikael's death last night, and she'd been sucked into the dream with him. Like sleep paralysis, but worse. She'd finally managed to extricate herself from Jimmy's nightmare, drenched in sweat, chest heaving. She couldn't get out of there fast enough.

She'd come down here to clear her head. Clanked through the dripping system of corridors. And eventually, she'd come to a window of thick polycarbonate plastic set into a dead end. Her favourite spot in this entire godforsaken bunker.

The window looked out mostly on swirling blackness. About half a nautical mile out into that blackness, however, was the real reason this place was the perfect centre of operations for the Void Hunters.

The Void.

In the hundred years or so since the founding of the Void Hunters, here at the bottom of the Atlantic sat the single largest gate to the Void that they'd discovered.

Which made it the single largest threat to humanity, perhaps to reality itself.

Anastasia thought it looked beautiful. From this viewing window, it was no larger than the very centre of a matryoshka doll. An oblong, obliquely angled fissure in the surrounding blackness. The gate was limned in a rope of the most beautiful green Anastasia had ever seen. Radioactive, as if dredged from the brackish pools of Chernobyl and cracked open to the nuclear core. A writhing, pulsing, effervescent shade of chartreuse—almost the exact penetrating neon of Jimmy's eyes, in fact. Or rather, not Jimmy's, but the creature he sometimes turned into. The irony of bringing a werewolf into a place that couldn't withstand even a single breach was as thick as these walls—"Twenty-five hundred PSI," Sammi kept reminding everyone, again and again, like a schoolteacher drilling fractions, "Twenty-five hundred PSI!"—but Jimmy insisted he had his transformations under control.

Anastasia knew bullshit when she smelled it.

Jimmy's werewolf side was just begging to take over. You could see it in his haunted expression, his haggard five o'clock shadow, the hollows of his cheeks. He may have acted aloof and unaffected, with a suave, cool demeanour; and he may have dressed the part in his Bloomingdale's blazer and corduroy slacks. But Anastasia knew a hair-trigger when she saw one. Jimmy was just as raw and exposed as she was. But whereas her flareups were spikes of psychic energy, his came straight out of a horror movie.

And horror movies rarely have happy endings.

As she ran, she thought, *I'm in that horror movie now.*

The corridor she was sprinting down turned ninety degrees just up ahead, but she didn't slow down. Couldn't. Instead, she leapt, planting one boot on the wall and pushing with all her strength, thrusting herself through the turn without sacrificing too much momentum. She careened along the tunnel's new direction for a brief moment before regaining her balance.

From behind her, the sudden chorus of werewolf claws trying and failing to gain purchase on metal, then a yipping whine as the beast slammed into the wall.

Anastasia grinned grimly. Hopefully she'd just gained enough ground to reach the alarm before Jimmy's fangs could sink into her back.

Jimmy, stop, please!

In response, the whines morphed into a chest-rumbling snarl.

The werewolf was back on the hunt.

Nu, der'mo! she cursed, and urged herself faster, faster.

She was on her own, then. The whole team was

counting on her.

The whole world, possibly.

No pressure.

But she was wrong, she knew. There *was* pressure. Twenty-five hundred pounds of it, just waiting to come crashing down on her.

Usually, staring at the Void gate had the effect of calming Anastasia's tortured mind. The glowing green outline was pretty, yes, but it was the rest of it that she liked most: the ethereal, cerulean blue light of the crystals spotting the gate's circumference, set into the rock around it. It was those crystals that truly protected the world from the Void. Even now, you could see them doing their work: oily ropes of pure black, blacker than anything Anastasia had seen, so that it sapped the light from everything around it, bubbled out of the gate's fissure only to be turned back by the crystals' protective perimeter. If those crystals were gone even for a moment, those blacker-than-black tendrils of sludge would pull from the Void a cryptid menagerie more terrifying than any nightmare.

Seeing that the gate was under control always served to ease Anastasia's anxiety. Even this morning, as she gazed through the thick viewing window, she could already feel it scraping the residual film of Jimmy's nightmare from her skin.

Ana.

She winced. Nobody was supposed to be able to speak directly into her mind except for her brother. She swore, trying to ignore the call. Why did Mikael have to fall in love? Letting Jimmy past his mental barriers had the invasive side effect of building a back-alley psychic connection between all three of them. A sick love triangle she wanted no part of.

Ana!

She scowled, still staring out at the Void gate. Her mind projected a curt response back at him, wherever he was: *Leave me alone.*

You know I can't do that, Jimmy said.

She crossed her arms, feeling suddenly cold. *And why not?*

Because... Mikael wouldn't want me to.

She could feel Jimmy somewhere up there, perhaps just one level above, pacing the corridors, searching for her. *You have no idea what my brother would want!*

The rest of the team is worried, too, Ana, Jimmy said.

His voice, even in her head, was deep, rich, rumbling. She could feel her brother's comfort at the sound of it, like a psychogenic echo. It was enough to make her hate him.

You don't hate Mikael, Jimmy responded. He was getting closer now. *You love him. Just as I love him. Just as he loved us.*

You were just an infatuation, she hissed. Her heart spiked. She tried to slow her breathing, tried to stare out at the crystals and clear her mind. But it wasn't working. *Fucking isn't love. It's carnal. Animalistic.*

She felt him wince at her words, and it gave her a tight smile.

You're lashing out, Jimmy said after an extended pause. *That's okay. I'm here.*

And he was. She could feel him, in the corridor behind her. Tall, mid-thirties—so much older than her and Mikael—with a shaved head and chocolate eyes. He stepped closer.

Stop! she screamed.

His boots squeaked against the metal floor. The force of her command had sent an invisible barrier crashing toward him like a wave, slamming into his barrel chest and stopping him in his tracks.

That's okay, he said again. *I'm here. I'm not going anywhere.*

She kept her back toward him, staring firmly out into the water but no longer seeing the gate. Her vision burned with sudden salt.

I need you, too, you know, he went on. *We both lost Mikael that day.*

The breath evaporated in her lungs. She couldn't move. Jimmy's last words had sent her hurtling through time and space to that moment, that nightmarish moment. Anastasia, pushing desperately through the tourists packed like sardines in Times Square. Screaming for Mikael to stop, don't, you don't have to do this, *moy brat*, there's got to be another way—

And his smiling face, projected in her mind, as he did it anyway. He put up a bubble of force, containing himself and the bomb the Void Hunters had come to stop.

MIKAEL, NO—!

The blast lit up the sky with nothing but light: the bomb's destructive energy remained in Mikael's protective bubble like a supernova, swirling beautifully in the centre of the packed street without harming a single bystander. Mikael's parting words—*Ya tebya lyublyu, Ana*—then emptiness, as if that part of her, that indelible piece that was her familial connection, had been scooped out of her brain. What was left was a hole in the grey matter. It was an uncoupling, a severing, of a psychic link she'd clung to her entire life. Gone in a blinding flash.

Mikael.

The nightmare ended, her paralysis broken. Her knees, suddenly water, gave beneath her and she staggered forward, catching herself on the polycarbonate glass of the viewing window. The Void gate, a swimming spot of green in her vision, seemed to pulse in rhythm with her headache, and with her heart.

A hand rested on her shoulder.

"Ana, please—"

“NO!” she barked, shrugging the hand off. “Don’t call me that. Go away.”

“I won’t leave you, Ana.” His large hand gripped her shoulder again. “I’m here—”

“Don’t you get it? You’re not the one who should be here. It should have been *you* in Times Square, not Mikael. Not on his very first mission. But you ran off with your tail between your legs.”

“You think I don’t know that?” There was a lump in Jimmy’s voice now. “You think I don’t tell myself that every day?”

“So just run away! Isn’t that what you always do?”

“No. Not this time, Ana. I’m here—”

“Only he calls me that,” she whispered. Tears spilled down her cheeks.

“I know, I’m sorry. I spent so much time in his head, I forget—”

“You’re—not—” *—HIM!*

Her palms pressed flat against the window and she braced herself, screaming her mind out behind her. Jimmy’s hand was ripped from her shoulder, and his body hurtled through the air. It came to a thudding stop somewhere behind her. Then silence.

Anastasia gasped. What had she just done?

“Jimmy…?”

He didn’t respond. She was about to turn around, but something caught her eye. Something that brought down the full weight of what she’d just done.

The crystals. Out there standing guard over the Void. Their blue light had been snuffed out. And there was no denying who was responsible.

Her hand covered her gaping mouth as she stared in horror.

The strands of black sludge quested hesitantly out of the fissure of the Void. When no resistance came, they rippled outward and outward again, a swirling mass of Stygian slick that all but swallowed the crystals.

Then, slithering from the neon gate, out of some unimaginable world and into this one, came the tip of a tentacle.

"No, no, no," she whispered. "I'm sorry, I didn't mean it, please, come back, crystals, come back—"

And, amazingly, they did. They stuttered and sparked at first, jerkily, like a faulty wire connection; then glowed fully back into existence, stronger and stronger, cutting through the sludge like it was nothing.

Because it *was* nothing. Whatever that sludge stuff was—antimatter, ectoplasm, some other sci-fi bullshit—it was essentially harmless. The Void's gloopy discharge, constantly checking the crystals' protective barrier for weaknesses. It wasn't the end of the world if some of that stuff swam with the fishes.

That tentacle, however… that was the real deal.

She stood, rigid, staring desperately out into the trench, wishing against hope that the crystals had sparked back to life in time to force the tentacle back through the gate and into the Void. *Please... please...* She held her breath, her heart hammering, until the sludge cleared.

The tentacle was still there.

It had pushed out of the gate, past the crystals' perimeter, before they'd come glowing back. Whatever resistant force those crystals possessed, it was apparently useless once a creature from the Void broke the circle. Like a circuit breaker. The tentacle was free to slither out into this world... along with the otherworldly leviathan to which it belonged.

A low moan floated out of the darkness behind her.

Jimmy!

Eyes still on the slithering tentacle, Anastasia spoke, her voice husky with panic.

"Jimmy, we have a big problem."

His moan grew in response, then turned into a hacking cough. It was thick, meaty, almost like a hyena's. Heavy shuffling sounds from where he fell.

"Yes"—his voice rumbled impossibly deep, like a gator's—"we certainly do."

A snapping sound nearly made Anastasia jump. She spun around.

"No, no, no," she breathed. "Jimmy, not now, please, no... *o, boji moi...*"

In the low-watt light that blinked spasmodically through the corridor, Jimmy lay in a heap, squirming and writhing in pain. His body appeared to be tearing itself apart from the inside, cracking him open for some grotesque Cronenbergian horror show. There came the staggered chorus of snapping bone and cartilage over the steady undercurrent of tearing skin. Blood splashed down in heavy gouts before coagulating and refilling Jimmy's new shape as it knitted itself together, impossibly fast like a time-lapse video. In the flickering light of a single bulb, he reared up from the ground, his clothing sloughed off his body like snakeskin. His skull brushed the ceiling and he growled, his long snout and peaked ears throwing shadows along the walls. His forearms had pushed themselves out until they swung low, past his knees. Or where his knees once were. Now Jimmy rose from haunches, his padded feet angled steeply up then bent forward in the unmistakable anatomy of a dog's hindlegs. Still pushing out from all of his paws came shiny black talons an inch thick, scraping the floor as he staggered to regain balance. His human form, two hundred and fifty pounds of solid muscle, had been ripped apart, rearranged, and knitted back together, somehow doubling in mass, his newly grown pelt bristling with thick black fur.

Another involuntary gasp escaped Anastasia as her gaze lifted from his hulking form to his eyes. They were open, and focused, and trained on her. Black lips peeled back to reveal two rows of fangs steadily unsheathing themselves from their gums. Saliva pooled and spilled over, slicking his furry chest, which shuddered with a guttural growl.

"Jimmy," she whispered. "Calm down."

He dropped heavily to all fours and began to stalk forward.

"Jimmy, we don't have time for this."

But Jimmy wasn't home. In his place was a beast that certainly wasn't as dangerous as the one crawling out of the Void right behind her, but it would nevertheless enjoy the privilege of ripping her apart first. Even so, she could hear the deep pull of ocean water as the thing behind her emerged from the Void.

She had to warn the others. It was the only way.

Her mind whirred, clicking into place at the only solution available to her. It was useless beating herself up for not bringing a walkie talkie down here with her—something Sammi was always bugging her about—but what was done was done. At least she had *one* tool at her disposal.

"I'm sorry, Jimmy," she said, slowly reaching for her hip. "This won't kill you, but it won't be a mosquito bite either."

In one fluid motion, she swung up her semiautomatic handgun while switching off the safety, aimed, and pulled the trigger.

The bullet hit his left flank, causing him to favour his right leg and list to the side of the corridor, yelping. This, she knew, would afford her mere seconds. Without thinking, she forced herself to charge forward, straight at the werewolf. She leapt as high as she could with so little runway, just managing to plant one boot on his heaving side.

She pushed off, and then she was sprinting for her life and the lives of her team. She'd already lost Mikael and Doc. She was done losing family to the Void.

Behind her, the werewolf's whine stopped. Just over the pounding of her own heart came the wet lapping and snuffling sounds of a dog licking its own wounds. Good. Maybe he'd forget about her, narrow her problems down by one.

Her bootsteps echoed behind her as she ran, the gun sweaty in her hand. Her mind raced, too, as she tried to picture the layout of this place. After all her time spent down here, surely she could navigate these corridors and find the communications room. Every level had one, and she remembered from Sammi's boring protocol lectures that there should be some kind of alarm she could activate. Probably an open comms link so she could tell Sammi and Will and the rest of the bunker just how badly she'd fucked up. And maybe—oh, why hadn't she paid better attention?—some sort of safety measure she could employ to isolate this level from the others. Whatever good that may or may not do.

As she approached the first turn up ahead, the entire corridor shook. Lights exploded, plunging the entire level into complete darkness. The floor heaved beneath her, and in her blindness it sent her stumbling to her knees. A sonorous roar shook the walls like sheets on a clothesline stirred by a gathering storm.

Shit. That was the Void creature, seeing if anyone was home.

As Anastasia stared blindly, willing her vision to adjust, another sound reverberated down the corridor behind her, chilling the blood in her veins.

"*A-YOOOOOO-OOOOOO-OOO!*"

She spun around, falling further so that she was scrambling backward, gun still in hand, crawling away from that bloodcurdling sound as she stared after it.

Jimmy. Howling. He'd picked up her scent, and now he was on the hunt.

"Get up, Ana," she muttered to herself. "Get—*up*."

She did. For Mikael. For Doc. For those she'd lost, but also for Sammi, for Will. For Jimmy. For the living, that they may continue to do so.

———

The situation was looking desperate.

The werewolf was hot on her heels, so close he was starting to snap his jaws out at her as she ran, nipping at her back. Even if she tried to turn and shoot, he'd have her before she could let off a single shot. If there wasn't a bullet lodged in his flank already, he might have leapt for the kill.

The Void monster seemed to be keeping pace with

them as well. The walls groaned in protest of their structural integrity being tested, juddering and shaking. Rivets pinged like ricocheting bullets. Sprinkler systems burst, uselessly ejecting their flame-retardant foam all at once. Entire panels of flooring buckled into new terrain like tectonic plates, forcing Anastasia to take leaping strides lest she trip.

It was all too much for her head. A cacophony of screaming metal and groaning pipe systems that spiked into the exposed nerve that was her twin's severed psychic link. Her paranormal abilities had been unreliable ever since Mikael's death, but now, if she survived this, she'd be lucky if she could so much as cheat at poker.

None of that would matter if she died here and now, at the bottom of an Atlantic trench. At the teeth of her dead brother's werewolf boyfriend, or from a Lovecraftian monster from another dimension. Not exactly *Sophie's Choice*, but she still didn't like it. And yet, she was no closer to finding the communications room. She'd die in this labyrinth, her own personal Minotaur slobbering just behind her. Where was the fucking—

The walls suddenly branched out on either side, dumping her into a larger space. Her mind screamed at her: *An intersection!* And all at once, she knew exactly where she was. Without slowing down, she turned left down a branching corridor. It would eventually lead to a stairwell, she knew, but that destination only awaited her if she survived her first stop. A doorway loomed just ahead, along the righthand side of the corridor. A slice of sterile white light spilled from the open door, causing her heart to surge, galvanized. All communications rooms must share a power source separate from the rest of the bunker, which meant its systems would still be online. She leapt for it—

"Unnh…"

A claw as big as her head swiped at her, batting her body like a ragdoll. She tumbled uncontrollably over the threshold of the communications room, limbs akimbo. Her left leg snapped like too-dry kindling and she tumbled in a heap, skidding across the floor. The room's far wall finally ended her long flight from the viewing window, that glimpse into the Void already seeming miles and hours behind her, though it could only have been minutes.

The werewolf, having skidded past the door, retraced his steps and peeked his frothing snout into the room. He stalked inside on all fours, breathing heavily. His limp was barely discernible; he may have left a trail of blood at first, but the bullet wound had already self-healed, the skin regenerating and zipping closed, the only sign of a gunshot the blood still matting his flank.

She opened her mouth to speak, then stopped. The Void monster was still making its presence known, the bunker all around her protesting in every way it knew.

There was no time to waste.

From where she'd come to rest, beneath a console, her eyes darted around for the alarm. Surely, with all the noise the Void monster was making, someone in the upper levels had already been alerted to its escape through the gate—but then, why hadn't they activated the alarm? Maybe that was a good thing; maybe the creature's destruction of the bunker only *sounded* apocalyptic and all this was still salvageable.

There!

A big, impossible-to-miss cherry-red button on the wall to her left, snug behind a breakable glass case. That was it. She didn't remember everything Sammi told her about this room, but she seemed to recall something about that button meaning *All hands on deck.*

There was no use testing her weight on her broken leg: several inches below the knee, her tibia and fibula had snapped cleanly, the jagged tip of the former poking through her Lycra legging. Swallowing the pain, she began crawling along the base of the wall in the direction of the alarm.

The werewolf's keen eyes swivelled at her first movement. He lunged forward, jaws agape. Anastasia had just enough time to grab the chair in front of her and pull it into his path. Teeth mangled its back and armrest. Rusty wheels squealed and the useless chair crunched forward under the beast's weight. Anastasia cried out. She was pinned, a shish kebab for the werewolf's final meal.

"JIMMY, NO, PLEASE!"

He pushed forward, his jaws crunching the chair, inches from her face.

JIMMY! she screamed out with her mind, praying his predator brain would receive the message. *The others need our help! You're not a mindless beast—you're a Void Hunter. Remember what that means!*

The slavering teeth seemed to pause.

Remember Mikael!

Through a hole in the chair's wrecked backrest, one giant eye stared madly at her. That vivid, glowing chartreuse, shot with red. Was she imagining it, or was that eye suddenly staring down at her in… recognition? In a pain that could be called remorse?

Mikael, she said again. Hot tears spilled down her sweat-drenched face. *My twin brother… your lover… he loved us. He loved you, Jimmy.*

A keening howl gurgled at the back of the werewolf's throat.

He may be gone, she continued, her chest heaving with sobs she'd never let herself release before now. *But he died fighting for what he believed. He died as a Void Hunter. And right now, you and I deserve the dignity to do the same.*

That large canine eye—now she was sure she wasn't imagining it—was slowly shrinking. Shoots of chocolate brown appeared in the iris, like inkblots.

Before Anastasia could do or say anything more, the continuous groans beyond these walls compounded and morphed into the shriek and pop of something large and metallic being ripped asunder. Joining this came a mighty rush and roar that Anastasia knew could only be 2,500psi of pressure crashing down on them.

She was too late.

No, you're not, sister.

The words sent a jolt through her. The chair fell apart and crumpled to the floor as Jimmy continued his transformation, and there, standing over them, impossibly, was—

You're not real, she told her brother.

Mikael smiled. *Perhaps. But I'm here, sister. I always have been.*

Maybe it was shock setting in from her broken leg; maybe the tears starbursting her vision into shimmery fractals of light. But Mikael was there, just feet away, in the same clothes as the day he'd died… and also he *wasn't* there. She could see the wall and ceiling behind him, as if through the polycarbonate viewing window, see them soar outward and rip away. See the black ridged edges of a massive tentacle as it gripped the bunker pieces like a child ripping apart its playthings. Was he a ghost? Or just a manifestation of her grief, all in her head? Did it matter?

Focus, Ana, Mikael said. *It's not too late for you.*

The red button behind its protective glass case

seemed worlds away, further even than the Void itself. But just then, Anastasia became aware of something in her hand.

Her gun. In all the commotion, she'd somehow never let it go. It was a miracle she hadn't shot herself in the fall. Now it was time for that miracle to pay off.

Even as a mile of ocean slammed toward her, even as the entirety of the Void monster came into view—far larger than the thing they'd fought on Coney Island, far larger than anything she'd imagined—she raised her gun over Jimmy's shaking, prone naked body, aimed, and fired.

She didn't hear the glass case break, but she saw it. Didn't hear the klaxon blare of the alarm as it alerted the rest of her team. Didn't hear the guttural scream of the monster from the Void. All she heard was her brother, echoing his final words to her in life.

Ya tebya lyublyu, Ana.

I love you, Ana.

She smiled back at her brother, that phantom limb whole once more, closed her eyes, and Anastasia felt all that pressure finally release.

UNFATHOMABLE

BY MATTHEW STEVENS

"Professor?"

My earpiece squawks with a burst of static.

"Yes, Simon?" I flinch and grunt. The comms are on but, descending alone in the quiet of the water in my submarine, I tend to get lost in the wonders of the ocean.

Since securing my first research grant, I have scouted deep sea waters all over the globe, but the Caribbean has remained my favourite to explore. The crystal-clear water and the sheer abundance of ocean life always leave me in awe.

When I was a child, my father, an astronaut, and my grandfather, a geologist and palaeontologist, argued about which path I would choose for my life. I defied them both and became a marine biologist.

A smile spreads across my face as a rainbow of colour swims past the dome of my sub, reminding me I made the right choice. Barely a hundred metres down, and my visual log includes six species of sharks, spotted eagle rays, sunfish (descending, I assume, in search of food), pilot fish, yellowfin grouper, and blue tang. The range of colours and sizes so close to the surface is a constant surprise.

The comms screech again. I squint at the piercing sharpness of the noise.

"We got the results back from the mass-spec."

"Let me guess: there's too much iron in the rock, and we'll lose the radios once I enter the cave."

Static hisses in my ear. Simon doesn't answer. I let him have a moment.

"I'll take your silence as confirmation of what I postulated when we recovered the sample."

As a PhD student and research assistant, Simon has gotten used to the occasional incorrect hypothesis. It's part of the job, but what he doesn't like is when he's wrong, and I'm not.

"Not having comms makes me nervous, Prof. Especially if you're going to be traversing a cave system we don't know anything about." Simon's voice lowers in apprehension.

"Relax. I've taken Dorothy down on nearly two hundred dives, and we've investigated almost a dozen caves." I sigh and click the comms off to give myself a pep talk. "You've got this, Wade. You've built your professional and academic reputation on exploration and discovery." I pat Dorothy's control panel and take a deep breath before I depress the comms button again.

"I know. I just…" Simon trails off.

"Need to leave the diving to me," I finish his sentence for him. I tilt the pedal under my left foot forward with my toes. The nose of the sub points downward.

"Did you find Nemo yet?" Simon chuckles as he clicks off the comms.

"No, Simon, I didn't. That joke is stale. Not to mention, that type of damselfish doesn't even live in this area of the Caribbean." I pause. "But you know that." Sometimes, his sense of "humour" leaves much to be desired.

Dorothy and I continue to dive. The sunlight strains to follow this deep into the ocean. As I put more distance between myself and the surface, the colourful ocean life that surrounded me moments before dulls in colour. The bright yellows, blues, reds, and greens all fade to varying shades of grey.

Through the acrylic dome, I can see that I am close to my destination. A glance at the instruments confirms I'm approaching the magical number of two hundred metres. In a few scattered places around the globe, the continental shelf begins its very decisive drop-off at that precise number. My current dive location, a few miles north of Honduras, is not one of those places, but the shelf starts to fall away within about ten meters of that mark.

The combination of dulling colours and a desire to visually confirm my destination prompts me to flip a switch, kicking on Dorothy's two large front-facing LEDs. My eyes adjust and return the colours to the ocean floor which moments ago seemed lost.

"Simon?" I call over the comms.

"What's up?"

"The entrance should be below me, so it won't be long before we lose radio communication. We should double check the instruments, gauges, and sensors." I scan the control panel in front of me.

Simon holds the channel open while clicking away on the surface far above me. "Checking over that now, Prof. Everything appears to be in order. I'm getting temperature and currents data from Dorothy's exterior sensors. Readouts indicate you should have enough oxygen for a two-hour spin through the caves and an hour's worth of air for your ascent."

"Excellent." I scan the control panel. Depth gauge, compass, and O_2 on my left, sonar, temperature, and comms on my right. "I'm seeing the same readings. Based on sonar and our preliminary dive, I'd bet about twenty metres to the cave mouth." I tap the multi-purpose screen in the centre of the console. Making a reverse pinching motion with my thumb and forefinger, I zoom in on my map.

"I'm showing you the very edge of the shelf."

I tilt my toes forward gently, increasing Dorothy's

speed. "I can't quite make out the edge. It must be just past the reach of the lights. Once I'm over the edge I'll rotate one hundred eighty degrees, descend a few more metres, and I should be looking at the cave."

I select the rear fins, and with my hand on the joysticks, I lift my toes, push my heel against the floor, and bring Dorothy around to face the continental slope. I release air from the ballasts, sinking until I'm even with the cave entrance. My second time seeing it brings a whole new set of emotions. I dove down yesterday to scout the location and cave opening. Knowing I'm going in and without comms, the jittery excitement of discovery is shrouded in uncertainty.

I give the pedal controlling the propeller speed a nudge, bringing Dorothy's nose right to the opening. "I'll have no trouble getting her in, Simon."

"We still should have taken more exact measurements. If you make it in and then get stuck, it'll be a close call on air before we can get a rescue sub down to you." Simon is a perpetual worrywart. If we don't account for every possible eventuality, he isn't satisfied. *If we planned for everything we'd never experience anything.* A proverb my father and grandfather lived by.

I hold my tongue. I say a silent prayer.

The opening in the rock face is a jagged and distorted grin behind which stalactites and stalagmites perch, imposing and ominous, like rows of shark teeth. In the back of my head, I can hear my grandfather say, "*You must think about the big picture, not just what you see in front of you.*" I smile. He was right. The rock formations, which can't form underwater, pose a challenge for me and Dorothy, but they also mean at some point, likely not long ago, this cave was not submerged. A realization that tempers my anxiety and ignites my curiosity.

I ease the joysticks to the side while tipping my toes forward to push Dorothy into the cave. Unconsciously, I make the sign of the cross over my heart. The acrylic dome has metal cross-braces for support and protection in these types of situations, and the sub's hull boasts carbon steel plating. As long as I don't bullrush the protruding rock formation, I should be able to weasel through without incident.

The comms squawk, and Simon's voice erupts in my ear. "I've set an alarm on your O_2 tanks. When you've got an hour and a half left of air, you'll get a warning, and then again when you hit that hour mark."

"Thanks," I try not to sound irritated.

"You're welcome. I know how easy it is to be caught up in the exploration and discovery."

"Simon." I can't hold back the indignation in my voice.

"Yes, Wade." He only uses my first name when he knows I'm aggravated and he's crossed a line.

"How many dives have we done?"

"Nearly two hundred."

"And how many times have I cut it close on oxygen?"

A pause. "Once."

"Thank you, Simon." I hold the button on the comms longer than necessary, emitting a jarring burst of static.

Dorothy glides past the initial cave opening, bringing me to the gauntlet of stalagmites and stalactites. I twist the joysticks gently, shifting left, then right, dodging. The dance is dangerous, but everything I've ever found worth exploring under the surface has always held an element of risk.

I float a little too far one direction, and out of the corner of my eye, I see the tubular metal dome support about to clip a stalactite.

Jerking the joysticks back the other way, I attempt to limit the damage. Dorothy quivers. The rock groans. I curse under my breath. Moments too late, we scoot away from the stalactite, which remains attached to the cave ceiling. A quick peek confirms that the metal support is sporting a good-sized dent.

I'd almost made it through unscathed. "Great. Now I'll have to deal with Simon smirking until we get back home," I grumble.

The cave groans again ominously as the stalactite I just bumped breaks free. It sinks in slow motion, but I don't have time to react. Dorothy jostles down and to the side as the rock connects with the acrylic dome. A hollow pop sounds, as a large crack appears in my plastic protection from the dark, impermeable world surrounding me. I curse under my breath.

I peer up at the ugly jagged scar in the acrylic shell and resist reaching up to run my hand across it. The shell is composed of two layers, and only the outer is cracked. I take a deep breath and focus on my surroundings. I'm here to explore and discover. Constantly checking and worrying about the dome isn't going to change what has already happened. Besides, seeing no bubbles escaping confirms that the pressure and seal are still intact. There are less than half a dozen stalactites to avoid before proceeding into the recesses of the cave. I skirt around those effortlessly.

The cave goes dark and quiet as I turn off Dorothy's LEDs and sonar. I take a deep breath and lean back in my chair, hands and feet off all the controls. My heart slows as my breathing steadies. Call it superstition or insanity, but I do the same thing in each underwater cave I explore. Sitting in the dark silence gives me a feel for the environment.

If not for the glow of the control panel, I would be able to see nothing at all. Regardless, I can see nothing past Dorothy's nose. Looking left, then right, I can't even make out how far I am from the cave walls. I double check the depth gauge. Two hundred seventeen meters. If I didn't know any better, I'd think this was the bathypelagic zone instead of the mesopelagic zone.

Only minutes ago, the crystal-clear water of the Caribbean and the colours of vibrant ocean life surrounded me. Now, it's as if I have sealed myself in my own coffin.

The comms screech, and I attempt to jump out of my seat; the harness keeping me securely in place digs into the soft skin between my neck and my shoulder. I reach up and rub the burn left by the nylon seatbelt.

Radios shouldn't work inside the cave, so either I'm getting interference from something in the cave, or Simon thought he'd buzz me before I venture in too far.

Assuming the latter, I depress the button to answer him. "Simon, do you copy? I've entered the cave."

The only answer I receive is static. I won't know until I exit the cave and head back to the surface if he registered my call. I think about all the times when my mother would call to me from the other side of the house. I would respond, but never loud or clear enough to be heard and understood.

If I turn around as far as I can manage, I still see the outline of the cave mouth. Despite being no more than fifteen meters behind me, the hazy light that permeates this deep into the ocean is too scant to illuminate the inside of the cave. A gentle beep from the sonar reminds me that I am wasting precious discovery time startling myself.

I flip the switch for Dorothy's headlights and blink as my eyes adjust to the light. As the wall of the cave in front of me comes into focus, Dorothy gently rocks sideways, and a trail of bubbles appears at the edge of my vision.

I gasp, my mouth falling open. "Interesting. There might be some ocean life in this cave system." The bubbles are a sign of life I'm pleased to see. My assertion that I would find something of interest here is what garnered me the grant money for this trip. Bringing back photographic evidence would further validate my expedition.

Cueing up the exterior cameras, I drive forward and scan my entire field of vision for a clue as to what jostled me. With the joysticks, I turn Dorothy all the way around. There is no sign of what might be swimming with me, but on the wall I notice indentations. Stopping my rotation, I nose her to the cave wall. What at first appear to be ancient tool marks transform upon closer examination. The deep gouges in the rock are neither simple nor arbitrary. There are three—no, four—sets of marks. In a very archaic sense, they appear stylistically reminiscent of logograms, each a series of parallel or intersecting lines, some with cyclical accents, but still seem different from those characters. *Could these be from before the cave was submerged?*

I turn Dorothy another few degrees horizontally to see if there are other characters carved elsewhere into the cave walls. At the edge of the headlights, I catch a brief reflection. Releasing the controls, I let Dorothy drift in the wake of her own movement.

As the light fully encompasses the creature, I recognize the distinguishing bell shape and large, oblong, ear-like fins of a vampire squid. The cephalopod flexes its eight webbed arms just before ejecting a cloud of bioluminescent cyan ink and propelling itself off into the dark. My jaw goes slack. I check the depth gauge. There it is in black and green—two hundred eighteen meters.

"But how?" I wonder aloud. Vampire squid have been recorded closer to the surface, but not commonly. *It must be the darkness that's appealing.* My pulse quickens as I consider what else I might find living—surviving—maybe even procreating in these caves.

These discoveries could be ground-breaking. My father liked to argue that he became an astronaut because space was infinite and therefore held more mystery than anything to be found on our already populated planet. My grandfather would always disagree, pointing to his own discoveries, hidden deep, buried in the secrets of the past. For my part, the ocean and its cracks, crevices, and caves, like my current situation, hide more than enough mystery to occupy me for lifetimes.

The vampire squid disappears into one of a dozen or more passages scattered around the room. I flip the switch to trigger the sonar and probe this initial cavern.

Most of the tunnels leading deeper into the cave system are too small for Dorothy to patrol, so I pick one of those remaining and gently drive her forward.

The passageway I choose descends then rises. It's like riding a surface wave. Each ascent and descent keeps me within five or so meters of the initial depth at the cave entrance. I continue the up and down for quite a while before noting that I've seen no signs of life since leaving the first chamber.

The repetitive rising and falling of the passage finally levels out, only to be replaced with twisting and turning. Left, right, left, repeat. After a few hair-pin turns, I find myself in a straightaway, and sonar can't pick up its terminus. I am only a few dozen meters down the straightaway when a ping echoes inside the cabin. Again. And again. At the edges of the lights, I see dozens of small offshoot passages. All too small for Dorothy.

Coming to a stop and twisting the joysticks to the side, I pull her nose even with the entrance to one of these side tunnels. On the left of this small passage, I notice another series of gouges in the rock. Not the same characters I found before, but the similarities indicate they are of the same language. This does little to shed any clarification on meaning or significance. Only with a thorough search and catalogue of these caves could I hope to draw conclusions from these markings.

A twist of a knob focuses the sonar. The computer

relays the information to me via 3D image. My eyes go wide. *That can't be right.* I tweak the sonar controls. The image flickers but doesn't change.

The passage in front of me is short, only a few metres long, ending in a rectangular room, which appears to house two objects. I enlarge the image and squint. Located at the top corner of the room one appears to be short and broad, almost square in shape. The other is long and thin and is floating, close to the opposite wall. Without thinking, I reach over and flip off Dorothy's LEDs. I reach across the panel and turn a knob which dims the glow from the control panel.

I blink a few times as my eyes adjust, leaning as far forward as the harness straps allow. A dull turquoise hue emanates from the corner where the squarish object is located. Almost as if multiple vampire squid projected their bioluminescent mucus simultaneously.

"What's down there?" I grunt in confusion. Grabbing Dorothy's joysticks I twist her around to face another tunnel situated behind me, repeating the process with the sonar.

Just as the image appears in front of me, something slams into me from behind, snapping my head back and shoving Dorothy against the opening of the small passage. Instinctively, I jam my arms up against the acrylic dome, trying to maintain its structural integrity.

"What the hell was that?" Some creature other than a vampire squid calls this cave home. Has to be. Not even a hundred vampire squid swimming at top speed could push Dorothy with that kind of force. My heart pounds in my ears. I force myself to take a deep breath. Then another. *Unless a shark is going to take a bite out of the hull, I'm safe.* Dorothy isn't impenetrable, but she's strong enough to withstand most predators I'm likely to encounter.

I wipe my sweaty palms on my pants, take hold of the joysticks, and spin back around. A new 3D sonar image appears on the screen with the tap of a few buttons. The square-shaped object is still where I left it, but the other, larger one has disappeared.

"Oh, my God! I have to find it. This could be the find of the century." My breath quickens. I try to imagine what this—thing—could possibly be. I have to find it and record its existence. My tape recorder is directly in front of me, attached with Velcro to the seal between the acrylic shell and Dorothy's hull. I press the little round red button.

"Professor Wade Magellan. It's the 28th of June. I am currently piloting my one-man submersible, Dorothy, roughly two and one-half miles off the northern coast of Honduras. On a cursory expedition yesterday, I discovered a cave that had not yet been registered on any official research maps. Today, I travelled back out to explore the cave and any connecting systems of tunnels and passages. My partner Simon and a hired captain are monitoring from a surface vessel."

I repeated the details I'd noticed thus far about the cave mouth, the inscriptions on the cave walls, and the appearance of the vampire squid.

"The sonar readings I took no more than three minutes ago showed what appeared to be a creature of substantial size occupying a small room off the main passageway of this cave system. With my back to the tunnel, it seems I was rushed by the creature, which is currently avoiding my detection. I am going to continue forward as I attempt to locate the creature, obtain photographic and/or video evidence, and classify it."

Pointing Dorothy's nose away from the cave entrance, I increase my speed and glide down the tunnel, ignoring the sonar pings indicating side passage after side passage. Logically, my brain urges me to stop and inspect another passage or two. For all I know, the creature could have swum into the very next alcove. Every few meters, I check over my shoulder. Nothing but blackness. I follow the straightaway until arriving at an intersection where I pull back on the throttle and contemplate my options.

"I have resisted the urge to check any other of the side passages peppered down the straightaway. The pattern of regularity with which the passages appear leads me to believe the unbelievable." I swallow hard, barely believing what I am about to say into the recorder. "It seems to me that whatever creature I'm searching for may be a highly intelligent life form."

The depth gauge reads two hundred twenty-two meters, a little deeper than the cave mouth, but not much. I emerge from a long passageway. *How close I am to being under the mainland?* Neither piece of information is critically important but tracking down whatever is living down here is.

Left or right? Back isn't an option. I turn the sub left and try to focus on whatever might be down this branch. A couple metres down the way, there is a faint blue-green shine like the one from earlier. I pull the joysticks, spinning Dorothy to face the other tunnel branch. Dorothy hasn't even come to rest before I see a substantial glow emanating from a room no more than ten metres away.

"At the end of the initial passage, I reached a three-way junction. My official scientific reasoning for choosing the path on the right is due to the significantly greater illumination from what appears to be a room not far from my current location. Proceeding to determine the source."

I aim Dorothy down the right branch. Barely a metre in, the search lights on Dorothy's hull flicker and go out. Flicking the switch back and forth a few times is a futile attempt to get them back on. They refuse to cooperate. Frustration gets the better of me as I pound my fists on the metal edges of the control panel. Sweat beads up on my forehead as my heart rises back into my throat.

Looking around I realise that the eerie blue-green glow is bright enough to guide Dorothy safely down the passage. *Getting out of here could be interesting.*

I begin to formulate a plan on how to exit without headlights when Dorothy is shoved sideways, scraping her hull against the rock wall. The screech of metal on rock sends my entire body quivering. I look up in time to stare in awe as a long, steel-blue creature glides past me around the corner, disappearing into the cyan effulgence. I can distinguish precious little about the creature as it swims away from me at speed.

This creature could be the same that burst out of the room pushing past me earlier, or it might be what left the mysterious trail of bubbles after I first entered the cave. Either way, my destination lies around the corner. Following the creature.

The intensity of the eerie glow grows as I drive Dorothy forward. The short passage opens into another cavern. As I approach the opening, everything is bathed in blue-green as if someone used glow sticks to paint every surface. This new cavern is not as large as I first presumed. There are multiple lanterns suspended from the ceiling. The intensity of the light unsettles my stomach. As I continue to scan the room, my eyes stop on two large creatures facing away from me.

Based on the hue of their skin, I'm sure that they are the culprits that shoved past me. I lean forward, wanting a closer look at these creatures, but I simultaneously lift my foot off the thrust pedal. The last thing I want is to draw unwanted attention. One of the first rules of exploration is to observe without disturbing, if possible. I'm so focused on examining these creatures that I crack my nose against the acrylic dome.

"Ungh." In surprise, I slam myself against the back of my seat. My eyes go wide, and I clamp my hand over my mouth. Now is not the time to grab their attention.

I wait, watching to see if they make any movements to turn around. Satisfied I haven't disturbed whatever they are doing, I lean forward again—more carefully, this time. Their grey-blue skin is comprised of scales. My eyes take in the spiked fin, reminding me of a bluegill, which begins at a crest atop each of their heads and runs to the base of the skull before rising again along their backs like a proper dorsal fin. I notice a mammalian-type head and human-like arms, so I expect legs. Instead, they each sport a lengthy tail that conjures images of classic mermaids from cryptozoology textbooks. I realize that the total length of each creature is greater than Dorothy, from nose to prop.

From my current location, I know there are details about these creatures that I can't discern, but their size and my recollection of how easily they brushed Dorothy aside make me hesitant to get closer.

Most creatures residing in the dark depths of the ocean rely on one of two mechanisms in order to see: either they produce their own light via bioluminescent appendages or sections of their bodies, or they have oversized eyes used to capture every bit of light. These creatures don't appear to have the former, and until I observe their faces I can't know if they rely on the latter. But, if such is the case, why the lamps?

Against my better judgement because I can't get a clear view of the source of the eerie glow, I tip the pedal, generating the smallest amount of propulsion Dorothy can eke out. Just enough to get her whole frame into the room and spin to face one of these lanterns. I don't take my attention off the creatures, but my tiny shift forward doesn't disturb them. Hands on the joysticks and a little tap to the side, and Dorothy rotates left.

The ear-piercing sound of the ballast tank scraping against the rock wall makes me cringe. In the same fluid motion, both creatures spin around, their gaze locking on to mine, tucked inside Dorothy's acrylic shell. I gasp and feel myself contracting muscles below my waist in hopes of maintaining control of my bodily functions.

Any comparisons to humans end at the shape of the creature's upper bodies. I stare back at their glassy black eyes, situated near the front edges of their skulls. My question about how they saw wasn't entirely unfounded. Their eyes are larger than one would assume based on the size of the skull, but smaller than living in the darkness of the ocean often necessitates. Two fish-like mouths rhythmically open and close as they suck in water to push past gills that I was unable to see before they turned. The description that pops into my head is "mermen".

Neither creature moves. They examine me as I do the same. Behind them I see a container glowing an intense shade of the pale blue green currently lighting the room. Just above that, there are three more sets of symbols scratched into the wall. It is obvious they belong to the same character set as the others, but they still bear no indication of meaning. I have yet to encounter any repeated characters. Then, to the right of the container I recognize the unmistakable shape of a human body. As horror engulfs me, I make out a mop of hair that floats limply, reminding me I'm still deep underwater. Empty sockets stare vacantly at the ceiling.

My breathing becomes shallow as I fight the onsetting panic. There is a familiarity to the body behind these creatures. *Why do I recognize that face?* I shouldn't. Simon and I have only been in Honduras a couple of days. I want to close my eyes and concentrate, but fear of what these creatures will do keeps my gaze locked on them. Then, like a wave crashing into a boat, the recognition rocks me. The news channels at the airport reported that a local professional surfer disappeared during last weekend's competition. They presumed him dead but still hoped to recover the body.

Too late for that now. But what are these mermen doing to him? As if in response to my unspoken question, the creature on my right turns around and returns to his previous exploits. However, the one on my left flips his tail and, in half a heartbeat, glides across the room, slapping his front fins on Dorothy's nose cone. For the second time in as many minutes I push my body to remain calm.

I glance at the merman by the surfer's body, then back toward the one only feet and a protective shell away from me. It's gone. My eyes are drawn back to the table. I watch as the merman dips a bony spike into the glowing container, removes it, and with expert precision slides it under the skin of the dead surfer's face. I watch as the merman repeats the process a second time. The third time he glides the spike into the surfer's arm.

The merman continues his work. I notice that the surfer's head, hair included, is now emitting the same iridescence that lights the room we're in. My breath catches in my chest. The air around me chills while my body begins to sweat. I pull my attention from the shocking procedure on the table and find one of the lights suspended from the ceiling.

I squint, trying to see through the glow. The shape slowly comes into focus. There hanging from the ceiling, emitting a ghostly radiance, are the remains of a shark attack. The longer I stare, the easier it is to make out the details. One leg is missing. A jagged semi-circle from the abdomen is gone. I turn to the lantern on the other side of the room. A rain hat and slicker are distinguishable. The body rotates and I see the logo from a fishing vessel emblazoned on the back of the slicker. A fisherman.

Panicking, I slam my hand on the button for the comms. *SCRREEAACHH!* I hit the button again, but the damage is done. I can't reach the surface, and I'm left with an intense, disorienting ringing in my ears. I have no way of knowing how many of these creatures live here or how long this torturous mortification has been occurring, but I can't sit and watch. Once I get back to the surface I will contact—someone.

I grip the joysticks and slam my foot on the throttle, spinning one hundred and eighty degrees. Dorothy barely fit down the tunnel the first time and she's blocking most of the light as I try to guide her back out of the room.

Metal crunches behind me and before I can adjust the controls, Dorothy's protective acrylic shell smashes into the wall above the room's exit. The previous crack erupts in a spiderweb pattern across the entire shell. Another crunch rattles Dorothy from behind. Again, the acrylic shell connects with the wall, this time obliterating the outer shell and fracturing the inner. A string of profanities escape my lips. Water begins running in rivulets along the curvature of the shell to the seal before dripping onto my elbow and the arm of my chair.

Each heartbeat thumps in my ears as I yank on the

controls and jam my foot on the throttle, desperately hoping to steer Dorothy out of the room. I try not to think about the lengthy tunnel, the zigzags, crests and falls that I must manoeuvre without external lights.

A hammer-like fin bangs down on the shell. The stream turns to a spray, saltwater splashing in my eyes and soaking my feet. I'm pressed forward against my harness as Dorothy is wrenched back into the room. Rubbing my face on my shoulder I try to clear my vision. Both mermen have webbed hands splayed across the shell. Their black, glossy eyes watch my struggle.

I reach up, pounding with my fists on the shell. Deep down, I know it's only bound to weaken the shell and make the water flow faster. Still strapped into the five-point harness I torque my body, struggling for the emergency dive gear. I can't reach. All I have is fear.

Shoving the throttle all the way down. Dorothy's propellers whine behind me, but I don't move. I search the cabin for something, anything, that might elicit an idea—a chance for survival. The water sloshes around my waist.

"Help me!" I plead with the mermen, clawing at the seal, desperate to escape. They share a look. They hear me. The inner acrylic shell has weakened, and water is coming from every direction. I know the water isn't actually freezing, but it's cold enough to suck all the warmth from my body. Shivers send the ripples outward from around my shoulders.

The shell shatters as I uselessly throw my hands up to protect my face and head. Water crashes down.

"Please!" I sputter into the cold saltwater.

They do nothing.

I fight for one last breath before submersion.

They watch as the water engulfs me.

My world goes black.

LIGHT THE WAY

BY MEGAN KIEKEL ANDERSON

According to legend, we were once beautiful. Down below the photic zone—under what is, to you, immense pressure—in the cold dark, our fellow creatures were mythical monsters, horrors adapted to survive.

Who among you would have been able to dream up the angler fish, all body spikes and grasping sharp teeth, its lure of glowing bacteria like something out of one of your science fiction novels? You aren't the only creature who fishes for prey. You certainly didn't know what to make of it when the first one washed ashore in the last epoch. We hope the thought of them frightened you, of seeing them swallowing their prey whole.

Had you imagined one large enough to capture your kind? If only that could have been. We find joy imagining you trapped in her maw. But even the black sea devil, as you called her, could not survive you. Their burrows on the sea floor may have been their undoing.

Most of the creatures down here would have terrified you even then—except perhaps the living fossil *nautilus*—blessed be their memory. Unchanged for hundreds of millions of years, they too could not survive you.

Somehow, we are what is left.

We, glowing bioluminescent, with our cartoonishly large saucer eyes, were the darlings of the deep.

We're different now.

How we outlived our predators of old, we can't say.

Well, not all of our predators. We know you ate our kin in the higher reaches, but don't imagine this to be revenge for that. We mourn the anglerfish, after all. This is not about the food chain. This is about genocide.

We didn't know much then, despite spending most of our time in school (excuse our little joke), and we're not sure we would trade this knowledge to recapture that beauty. But we might relinquish it not to be born in pain. Now we are as nightmarish as our fellows would have seemed to you.

Not all of us made it to this age, of course. Our fellow species of lanternfish made up something like sixty-five per cent of all deep-sea biomass when the

Anthropocene, the age of *you*, began to encroach on our world. Now our species is all that is left, though we shudder to think of what percentage of living creatures of the deep we now represent. So many have been lost to us.

You cannot deny you are at fault. We are told tales of the age of old from the time we are spawned. Before you, we were minding our own business, shoaling together, basking in the glow of our community. Courting, feasting on zooplankton, enlightening the eternal dark. We were simply fish, not monsters.

The closest thing you could consider a crime by our kind was simply a matter of confusion. Oceanographers were perplexed by sonar scans when our gas bladders created a "false bottom," a deep scattering layer that made you think the depths stopped with us.

If only our unintended ruse could have stopped your byproducts from reaching the true bottom. Alas, you learned your mistake, and our glowing could do nothing to stop your microparticles from sinking to our world.

How could we, so unoffending, deserve such a fate?

But of course, your villainy, for all of your supposed knowledge, is in your thoughtlessness.

You began to spend more and more time in the deep, your submarines, to our eyes, a strange cyborg fish imitation.

We listened. And we learned.

Your instruments delivered to us knowledge of seascapes afar. You collected information like an octopus collecting stones for their seabed garden.

Yet you used material that will last a millennium to cover a single morsel. No perspective, no perspective at all.

It should have drowned you. But instead, you tried to bury it under your land, letting it flow into the sea. Sure, some evidence of your crimes was visible to you. You ruined your beaches, playgrounds of mating rituals and relaxation. You made islands of refuse that could not be ignored.

But most of it, battered by sun and salt and wave, sinks down and down to our realm. We eat more plastic than zooplankton now. The deep sea floor is no longer made of sand.

It's part of you now too. It's in everything you eat and drink.

You are the monsters of this story, but come the dawn of the next age, if we can't stop you, you must mutate yourselves into monsters too. We are no longer darlings, but we won't be alone in that.

According to our scholars, all hope for life is not lost.

At the vents of the East Pacific Rise, where the tectonic plates meet, you'll find the hub of the creation of new land, an inferno shooting from the trenches. You thought no life could be found in such a place, noxious chemicals rising from the center of the Earth, heat matching the days on Mercury, somehow otherworldly to you though it is deep within our own planet.

The bacteria there photosynthesizes from the infrared light given off from the heat. It metabolizes using not oxygen, but hydrogen sulfide. Where you expected to find nothing, life flourishes.

What can your poison do to life that thrives in such a world?

Your scientists believe that this alien hellscape on Earth may be where all life began.

It can flow forth from there again, this time adapting to the poisonous underwater wasteland you've created.

Our time is done now. And so is yours.

Now, we rise.

For the bigfin squid, we rise. For the nautilus, we rise. For the whalefish, we rise. For the sperm whale, we rise. For the hagfish, we rise. For the giant isopod, we rise. For the giant squid, we rise. For the oarfish, we rise. For the gulper eel, we rise. For the hatchetfish, we rise. For the coelacanth, we rise. For the sixgill shark, we rise. For the snipe eel, we rise. For the vampire squid, we rise. For the viperfish, we rise. For the giant tube worm, we rise. For the anglerfish, we rise.

FOR THE LANTERNFISH OF OLD, WE RISE.

For what is left, we light the way.

JULIA

BY ANDREW CULL

On March 1st 1999, National Oceanic and Atmospheric Administration (N.O.A.A.) hydrophones recorded an underwater sound so loud it was heard across the entire Equatorial Pacific Ocean array. That sound was dubbed, "Julia".

To this day, the origin of the Julia sound remains unknown.

Do you know how many lives the sea claims each year? How many bodies it swallows never to be seen again? Yes, we recover some, but how many more are lost to the darkness forever? Where else but a graveyard would you find so much discarded flesh?

Is it any wonder that its depths are filled with

monsters?

—

Sounds, taken out of context, can be open to interpretation, our life experiences framing how we perceive them. You heard claws scratching at your window, I heard the branches of the oak tree in our yard. You heard a scream in the night, I heard a fox crying in the fields by our house. I still hear your cries for help.

When I first heard the *Julia* sound, I knew exactly what it was.

—

March 5th 1999

"…Richardson's already written it off. Says it just sounds like another *Upsweep* recording. But, there's something different about this one. Doesn't sound like an iceberg running aground to me."

I wasn't listening. I refilled my glass. A cheap scotch blend that I'd picked up from the liquor store a block from our house. Cheap and large. The quickest possible exit from reality, please. I hadn't waited to get home before I opened it. Formalities are for people who don't really need a drink in the first place.

"Would you give it a listen if I send it to you?"

No.

"Tom? You there?"

I drained the glass and refilled it. "Send it over."

"Oh, okay, great. You've got the best ear in the acoustics business, Tom. I'll send the file straight away. Er…"

Here it comes…

"Look, Tom. I'm really sorry about what happened…"

I ended the call.

The world had been moving at a crawl ever since the accident. Time stretched taut over broken glass memories. Eventually something was going to tear. I don't know how long after the call I booted up my laptop, but Bob's email was waiting for me when I did. No subject, no message (too awkward), just a .wav file attachment.

I slipped my headphones over my ears, picked up my glass and hit play. The drink didn't make it to my lips. That was the first time I heard the voice.

———

March 7th

If you want to save the starving children, you can forget it. If you want to throw millions of dollars at Mars or the Mariana Trench, well, there's a billionaire for that.

Add in some naming rights for whatever you discover and you'll likely have a bidding war on your hands. We raised the funds for the expedition in twelve hours. Two days after Bob had sent me the email, I was the only passenger on a six-seater plane descending to land at the N.O.A.A. base at Cape Adare, Antarctica. I watched the black peninsula of the cape come into focus. A coastline of high, jagged, basalt cliffs spread across the otherwise perfect white landscape like a stain, like the inky corpse of some huge beast washed up from the ocean thousands of years ago. I couldn't think of a better place to begin the expedition.

In the two days since I'd received Bob's file, my headphones had barely left my ears. I'd listened to the recording hundreds of times. I'd filtered it to lessen the background noise, played it at different speeds to account for the ocean temperature and depth at which it was recorded. The sound had been picked up by multiple hydrophones along the N.O.A.A. array, which meant Bob had been able to triangulate it with some accuracy. His calculations suggested that it'd come from an area between The Bransfield Strait and Cape Adare. I guessed that was why Richardson had dismissed it as an iceberg grinding along the ocean floor. Had he even listened to it properly? There was no doubt it was organic. Maybe he and Bob hadn't recognized it because they hadn't heard it before. Maybe it was because it wasn't meant for them.

When you spend your life on the ocean, when you love it intensely, it can be easy to forget how callous it is. How insignificant we are to it, how out of place on its surface, or in its depths. It wants nothing more than to consume us, to drown and devour us. When our yacht capsized, I was on the main deck, my wife and daughter in the cabin below. Maisie had always been scared of confined spaces, made us keep the cabin door open whenever she was below. That was how the sea got in so fast.

You don't just hear a scream underwater, you feel it too. As we touched down at Cape Adare, the recording swelled against my ears. I closed my eyes and pressed my headphones tighter. I felt the sound mixing with the rush of my blood in my skull. I felt the cry in my heart.

Around me the plane juddered and skidded to a halt. When I opened my eyes again the black cliffs towered all around me. The dark peninsula had consumed me.

March 8th

At its deepest point, the Bransfield Strait measures two kilometres surface to seabed. The largest iceberg in the world reaches between six and seven hundred feet down. That's only around two hundred metres into the sea. Given, the Strait isn't all as deep as its deepest point, but what chance was there really that the sound was an iceberg scraping the sea floor?

Our crew consisted of two deep sea acoustic technicians (Kyle Hillerman and Geoff Holt), an underwater videographer who'd been part of the '85 team who discovered the Titanic wreck (Conrad Janssen), an ROV operator (Kelly Blake-Peterson), the captain (Don Grosse) and his second, and a photographer supplied as part of our funding deal with our billionaire benefactor. Loading the ship took a whole agonizing morning, but by lunchtime on the 8th we'd set sail. *I've heard you, and I'm coming.*

———

It's hardly state of the art, given the value of each of the sonobuoys, but in order to deploy them you tie a sandbag to them and hurl them into the sea. The sandbag anchor drags the buoy to the ocean floor; a floating marker marks the spot of deployment for later retrieval. Kyle and Geoff began dropping buoys at five-mile intervals along the Strait. I sat below in the lab the jittering green line of the spectrum analyser screen, listening, and waiting. Kelly monitored the live data on her own laptop. If we got a good hit from the buoys, she'd deploy the ROV, piloted from a console across the table from me, to get a better look. Windows on either side of the cabin looked out onto the freezing waters as we carved a slow path along the trench.

March 10th

We were an hour from sunset when Geoff called through the hatch into the cabin:

"Bob, come take a look at this."

I hauled myself up the metal steps and onto the main deck. A layer of ice, sea spray turned to glass, made the upper deck treacherous. We trudged towards the bow, where Kyle was leaning, peering into the black water below.

"More here…" He pointed.

I looked over the side. A dead fish bobbed past my view. Then another followed it. I watched as five more slid along the side of the boat, bounced against the hull by the current.

"What are they?" I asked.

"Look like rockcod." Kyle leaned further over the

side.

"We've been seeing them for the past hour or so. Just one or two to begin with, then these groups of about ten." Geoff ran a hand over his beard; his glove came away covered in ice crystals.

"I wonder if there's been a chemical spill out here." Kyle was attempting to prod one of the fish with a hooked pole we used to drag buoys from the sea.

"That might explain why nothing's eating them." Geoff added.

"What do you mean?"

"Well, we've not seen a single predator, no birds circling, no seals, no larger fish. These rockcod are a free lunch and no one seems to want 'em."

"Christ!" Kyle had wandered around to the bow of the ship. He was looking out at the sea ahead of us.

"What is it?" called Geoff, but fish had already begun spilling along the sides of ship.

"G! G!" Kyle was frantically waving to Geoff to join him. I followed.

As far as we could see, stretching out across the Strait, hundreds of silver bodies swelled on the waves, rising and falling all around us. A thousand dead eyes staring forever more into the sky. A thousand dead eyes watching the last rays of sunlight draining from the day.

"Good God."

Or perhaps they were fixed on the depths beneath us.

"Tom! Tom!" Kelly called as she scrambled up onto

deck. “We’ve got a hit!”

Maisie’s hand had a way of appearing in mine. We might be walking along, or sitting on the deck of the yacht, and I’d feel her little fingers reaching across my palm, waiting for my hand to close around hers. She liked to hold hands, and I liked it too. She was only five, but she was smarter than her years, and fiercely independent. She already did so much without me or my wife. It was nice to feel that she was still my little girl for a while longer.

I sat at Kelly’s laptop, headphones pressed tight against my ears.

“Frequency’s really low,” Kelly noted, tapping at the spectrogram excitedly. “It’s loud, too. Big.”

I closed my eyes. *I’m here.* I listened.

I can’t think of a worse way to die. When our yacht capsized, the sea flooded the boat with such ferocity that it filled the cabin in seconds. I was on deck when the whole world turned over. As the yacht rolled, it dragged me underneath it. I was sucked into the darkness, past the cabin; I slammed into the bow and was spat out into the ocean.

I lay on my back, looking up into the perfect blue sky above me. I didn't know how I'd gotten there. My mouth was full of blood. I must have hit my head when the boat went over. I could hear frantic hammering but I couldn't tell where it was coming from. I turned to ask Maisie if she could answer the door, but instead I rolled into the water and it was her face I saw screaming against the glass of one of the cabin windows below.

I'd never seen fear like that. There was madness in it. My little girl who was afraid of confined spaces, trapped in the flooded cabin, small pockets of air above her growing smaller all the time. She thrashed and kicked at the glass, bubbles exploding from her mouth as she screamed.

I dived down until I was on the other side of the pane. I beat my fists on it until my knuckles trailed blood in the water. I managed to grab a hold of a rail above the window and swung my legs at the reinforced glass. My feet just skidded over it. Behind Maisie, I caught a glimpse of my wife. Her lifeless body buffeted in the wake of Maisie's thrashing.

The door! Maisie, swim for the door!

She insisted we kept it open when she was below deck. It'd been open when the boat had rolled. I hammered on the window, trying to get her attention, but she'd twisted away from the glass, pressing her face into an ever-shrinking pocket of air above her.

Please, sweetheart. Swim for the door!

I hauled myself along the upturned hull until I found the ladder into the cabin. As I did, I felt the boat shift. The bow dipped. The boat was beginning to sink.

I grabbed the handrail and launched myself up the stairs. I slammed into the closed cabin door.

NO! NO! NO!

It must have swung shut when the boat rolled. I threw myself against it, tried to force it with my shoulder. Bubbles of precious air swarmed around me, freed from the cabin, racing for the surface. There was a gap between the door and the frame! I forced my arm through, frantically swinging and snatching for whatever was holding the door closed.

My whole body screamed, screamed for air, screamed for Maisie, screamed into the darkness that was drawing over my eyes. I felt something brush against my hand, on the other side of the door. I grabbed at it and held it.

It was Maisie's hand.

I'm here, honey, I'm here.

The last air left my lungs in a sob.

I'm sorry.

I'm so sorry.

I held on tightly to her hand. It was so small, so still.

Please take me with you.

The boat was tipping, sinking fast now.

I held on for as long as I could.

I'm here.

"Some kind of mass mortality event..." I could hear Geoff explaining to Kelly about the fish. I pressed the headphones tighter to block him out.

I'm here.

The spectrogram danced, blue and red, streaming across Kelly's laptop screen.

"...HELP..."

It was heavily distorted, but I knew what I was listening for. In the first recording the voice had been too degraded to make out the words. I knew who it belonged to, though.

"...HELP US."

It was my wife's voice. Julia's voice.

The crew of a fishing boat had pulled me out of the water. I should have been dead, I wanted to be dead, but the sea, in its infinite cruelty, had spat me out again.

Coastguard divers were sent to retrieve Julia and Maisie. I sat on the deck of the response boat staring at my empty hands.

After a time, the divers returned. Something was clearly wrong.

The cabin was empty. They'd found the boat resting on its side on the seabed. The cabin door had been open. Whatever had been blocking it had likely been dislodged when it grounded.

It fell upon a red-faced young man to tell me the details. He assured me they'd continue to search until Julia and Maisie were found, but two days later the search was called off.

The whole thing was ruled an awful freak accident. No one was able to explain how a boat, piloted by an experienced sailor, had come to capsize on seas as calm as they were that July day.

The first recording had begun with my wife's voice. Too distorted to hear clearly what she was saying, but it was unmistakably her. It had ended with Maisie's scream, the two sounds converging on the spectrogram. Wherever they were, they were together.

Kelly stood at the map of the Bransfield Strait we'd taped to a whiteboard in the middle of the room.

"The first buoy is here." She drew a circle. "The second… here." Another circle. "Because we only picked up the sound on two buoys, we can't triangulate it accurately. My best guess, from a rough analysis of the data, is that it's coming from further up the strait. Ahead of us."

"And leaving a trail of dead fish behind it," added Kyle.

"What if it's not organic?" Geoff said.

"Sure looks like it is from the data." Kelly was taping a copy of the spectrogram onto the map.

"What if we're tracking some classified Russian sub? Maybe it's leaking something that's killing all the fish in its wake."

"If it is, great. We can ask them if they've got any good vodka on board, because fuck me, I'm cold and I could use a drink." Don toasted us with his coffee mug.

I excused myself and headed to my cabin. Kyle and Geoff would take it in shifts to continue to drop buoys through the night. They told me they'd wake me if we got any more hits.

In my room, I began to work on cleaning up the recording. The first pass through the software was going to take six to eight hours.

Almost a year before, I'd held my daughter's hand as she drowned, watched my wife's lifeless body sink to the bottom of the ocean. Now, somehow, Julia was calling to me, sending messages that had brought me halfway across the world to find her. I couldn't allow myself to follow that thought any further. Never finding their bodies, never being able to bury or say goodbye to my family, had broken me. I knew madness, knew that it coiled inside me. I'd seen it in Maisie's eyes as she thrashed against the cabin windows. I saw it in my own eyes whenever I glimpsed my reflection.

I stood at my porthole looking out. The corpses of hundreds of fish, picked out silver in the boat's floodlights, slithered past as we ventured deeper along the strait. Death pressed against the boat on all sides.

Tell me how I can help you. Tell me what you want me to do.

March 11th

"Tom. Tom, wake up." Kelly knocked on my cabin door.

In my dream, Maisie was hammering on the cabin window. I started awake. The knocking followed me out of my sleep.

Kelly called again. "Tom? Are you awake?"

I'd fallen asleep watching the progress of the recording being filtered. Ten per cent left to go.

I hauled myself off my bunk and opened my cabin door. "What is it?"

"Something you need to see."

I followed Kelly through the boat. Geoff and Kyle were waiting for us in the lab. It was obvious something had spooked them.

"Why aren't we moving?" I asked.

"You'll see".

Kelly led me over to her laptop. "Just before five A.M. we began picking up a new signal. Higher frequency that the last one."

"Something smaller?"

"Once every forty-eight hours, Don brings the boat to a full stop. Does an hour of checks before we head off again. It was about half an hour after he'd stopped that we started picking up the sound."

I looked at the spectrogram on the screen. "That's not organic."

"Right."

"But I was able to triangulate it. Because it was picked up on the last ten buoys we've dropped. At the same time."

"That's not possible."

"Just tell him, for fuck's sake," Kyle growled.

"Follow me."

Kelly led me up onto the main deck. The cold was startling.

"Look." She pointed over the side. I recognized the marker straight away, an orange ball bobbing on the surface. One of our sonobuoys was sitting about twenty feet off the starboard side of the boat.

Then her hand began to sweep to her right. Another orange ball bounced on the black water. She continued right…

Another marker, and then another. "They're all around us. The last ten hydrophones we dropped in the strait," she said. "The sound we picked up, it was us. We were recording us."

"Who's watching who here, huh?" Geoff said grimly.

It took most of the morning to haul back in all the sonobuoys. Kyle tried to suggest that maybe they'd gotten tangled, that we'd been dragging them as we'd been deploying them, but none of them were twisted together.

Geoff suggested sending Conrad or the ROV down to see if there were any signs of how the buoys had come to be circling us, but Don wouldn't have it. "We've lost enough time to this. Funding's only paying for a ten-day expedition. Losing a morning can soon turn into losing a day if we don't get moving."

He was right. I left Kyle and Geoff resetting the equipment and headed back to my cabin. Don followed me to my door.

"Can I talk to you?" He let himself inside.

As soon as I was through the door, he closed it. For

a long moment he stood looking at me, as if he was sizing me up, deciding whether or not to tell me what had brought him to my room. I noticed that my laptop had finished processing the recording from the night before. I turned it to face the wall, away from Don's view. It wasn't meant for him. "What's going on, Don?"

"I didn't stop the boat this morning. I just told your crew that," he said.

"What do you mean?"

"'Bout four thirty, I went to get coffee. Left Chuck at the helm. He's young, but he's a good second." Don shuffled, foot to foot, a surprisingly childish movement for such a large, and usually assured, man.

"Okay."

"I'd just made it to the galley when everything went off. The whole place just, snap, into darkness. Then I felt it".

Don looked at his feet again, only this time he was reliving what had happened.

"I thought, shit, Chuck's gone and grounded us, run us onto an iceberg. I could feel the grinding coming up through the hull, through my feet, into my legs. I dropped my mug and I ran." Don was talking faster now, his voice shaky. "Only when I get to the helm, there's no ice. Just the black water of the strait all around us. And Chuck. Poor kid's confused and scared half out of his mind. Says that just before the bow spotlights went out, he saw something in the water. Said it was just under the surface. A huge shape. Said it stretched across the channel as far as he could see. He thought it was rising, thought it was gonna hit us. That's when the grinding started."

"Did you see it?"

"No. I felt it though. Something scraping along the hull. I went up onto the top deck, and that's when I saw those buoys circling the boat. 'Bout ten minutes more and all the power came back on again. I've been running checks all morning, and there's no reason it should have been off in the first place."

"Where's Chuck now?"

"I gave him a stiff drink and sent him to his bunk to try and get some rest."

"You think he was mistaken?"

"Do you? What is it you're looking for, Tom? What do you think's out here?" Don's tone had changed. His fear had backed him into a corner. Now it was turning into something else.

"I don't know."

"You don't know, or you don't want to tell us?"

"I don't know."

"I trust Chuck. If he says he saw something, he saw it. Better hope, for all our sakes, that it was just a whale. If I think we're in danger, I'll turn this boat around, do you understand?"

You won't do that, Don.

I went straight from closing my door on Don to my laptop on my bunk. The recording had finished processing. Filtering the audio had revealed a peak of sound after the first two pulses (HELP US). A third band on a slightly different frequency: a different voice. Like the first recording, this one contained two voices. Maisie spoke after Julia. A single word: RISE.

HELP

US

RISE.

I dragged my cursor along the recording. I listened to Maisie's voice again. I closed my eyes and tried to picture my little girl. I hadn't heard her speak for almost a year. I hadn't thought I'd ever hear her again.

"I miss you," I said. My throat closed on the words. Tears streaked my face.

Even with my headphones on, I heard the screaming from above me.

I scrambled up the steel steps and out onto the main deck. It was Kelly who was screaming. Chuck was dragging her backwards, towards the bow, by her hair. One of his hands gripped a clump of her hair; he jerked and pulled at it as he dragged her. The other held what looked like a large shard of glass, pressed tight against her throat.

Despite the near freezing temperature, Chuck was only wearing a pair of shorts. His bare feet skidded over the slick boards, leaving a trail of bloody footprints as he staggered backwards.

Most of the blood was his. His bare chest and legs were covered in jagged gouges. A flap of skin hung loose from his abdomen, peeled away to reveal the raw muscle beneath. I was struck with the awful thought that he'd tried to flay himself.

Geoff edged up the deck after them, shaking hands held up in front of him to urge calm.

"For Christ's sake, don't fight him, Kel," he pleaded.

I passed Don, standing with a hand clamped over his mouth, utterly paralysed by what he was seeing. Chuck slipped and Geoff let out a small cry. He just managed to keep his balance, but blood had begun to run down Kelly's jacket where he'd nicked her.

"Chuck!" I called. "Chuck, let her go!"

"I SAW IT!" he screamed. "I SAW THEM!"

"Please." Kelly whimpered.

"What did you see, Chuck? What was it, Chuck?"

"There are hundreds of them. They're bringing it to the surface, raising it up."

Off the port side of the boat, the sea had begun to bubble, to churn. Could it hear us?

"Who are, Chuck?"

Geoff shot me a horrified look. I knew what he was thinking, but I had to know.

"*Who*, Chuck?"

"You know! You brought us here! You know!"

Chuck had dragged Kelly to the bow. They had nowhere left to go. Chuck pressed against the railings, his feet slipping over the deck as if he hadn't realized he'd reached the edge. He kept stepping, kept leaning backwards.

"Chuck! Please, stop!" Geoff pleaded.

Chuck stopped. He turned to look straight at me. Then with one terrible movement, he jerked Kelly's head back, raised the shard of glass high, and drove it down into her right eye socket. A jet of fluid and blood squirted into the air, it rained down over Chuck and the deck. At the same moment the sea lashed at the side of the boat, as if the water had risen to meet the gore. Chuck scissored down Kelly's cheek with the shard. He drove it in with such force that I heard it snap in the wound. Kelly clawed at Chuck's arm, at her face, flailing and screaming. He yanked what remained of the shard from her cheek—Don was crying out behind me, "NO, GOD NO!"—grabbed her hair once more and threw her over the side.

Geoff had collapsed onto his knees. He was crying into his hands.

Chuck rocked against the railing. He raised his head up, exposing his neck to the sea. Then he scored the shard across his throat, opening it up, spraying blood into the ocean. He collapsed forward, following Kelly into the hungry waters below.

I ran to the bow, skidding over the bloody boards. My hands grabbed at the railing to stop myself from following Kelly and Chuck over the side. The sea below was frothing, red foam splashing over the hull. I thought I saw an arm gliding just beneath the surface.

I grabbed one of the hooked poles used to drag in buoy markers, and jabbed it into the water. A pair of hands rose out of the red waves and wrapped around the pole. I felt their pull immediately, I was barely able to hold on. They were too small to be Kelly's hands. When I realized who they belonged to, I dropped the pole.

"Maisie!"

I tried to reach the pole, snatch it back, but it sank beneath the surface. I leaned over the rail, hooking my boots against the uprights so I could lean further out.

"Maisie! NO! MAISIE!" The pole disappeared below the waves.

As I watched, the whole sea seemed to darken. A huge shape was passing under the boat. It rose until I could see grey mottled skin. It rose until I felt it grinding along the bottom of the boat. Then it opened its eyes.

As far as I could see, the ocean turned to look at me. Hundreds of milky orbs, watching me from below the red foam, seeing me, seeing everything. I could feel their gaze inside my skull, as sure as jagged fingers burrowing into the darkness that grief had spawned there. They searched out my pain, my anger, and feasted upon it. All the time, a huge noise, static I couldn't decipher, swelled through me, louder and louder. I clamped my hands over my ears to try and block the sound out, to keep my mind from shaking apart.

I lurched against the rail, the creature's ancient eyes pulling me forward. My feet slipped free—Kyle grabbed at the back of my shirt and hauled me back onto the deck. I lay on the blood-streaked boards and screamed.

The shard that Chuck had used to murder Kelly had come from the mirror in his cabin. The rest of it had been reduced to a bloody mosaic in the sink below. This was where he'd cut himself.

"Christ," groaned Don. He looked like he might pass out at any moment. "Why the hell would he…? I mean I've known him for years… since he was a kid."

"Sit down, Don."

He slumped onto Chuck's bed and rested his head in his hands.

After Kyle had thrown me onto the deck, and I'd lost sight of the creature's eyes, the static had faded from my mind. It hadn't gone altogether though. I could still feel it in my ears, a constant vibration, a hum. The thing was still nearby.

Chuck had sliced patches of his skin from his body, discarding his flesh onto the floor around the sink.

“We have to turn back.” Don spoke into his hands.

“No.” I’d seen Maisie with my own eyes. There was no way I was turning around now.

“What? We’ve got no choice! You saw what happened. We can’t carry on!”

“No. We’re closer to the open sea than we are to Cape Adare. We go on. You want a rescue? That’s the way we go,” I lied.

Don got to his feet, fast.

“No! You don’t want us to get rescued.” He closed the distance between us, spat the words at me. “Chuck said it! You know what’s out there. You know what caused this, what made him do…”

His eyes were full of tears.

“This is my boat. I’m the captain, and I’m turning it around.”

“No, you’re not, Don.” I reached into the sink. I felt the glass slicing into my fingers as my hand tightened around it. I raised a shard and slashed it across Don’s throat.

I missed with my first strike, jamming the shard into his windpipe. Don stumbled backward, gasping, air whistling out from the wound with a sickening hissing moan. He threw up a hand to try and deflect my second slash but he was too slow and I connected with a vein.

He tried to grip, tried to cover the gash, grasp for the blood that was spouting from his neck. I slashed again and again, the static roaring in my ears. The hum had risen to a scream. The creature had returned to feed once more. I slashed until Don's legs buckled and he fell onto his backside on the floor. He sat for a moment, as his life pumped through his fingers and poured down his front. He opened and closed his mouth, trying to scream, but air just bubbled and gurgled out of his ruined neck.

I knelt down, my legs close to giving out too. "I'm sorry, Don. I can't turn back now." I dropped the broken mirror piece.

Don rocked over, crumpling onto his side. Moments later he was dead.

When Kelly and Chuck had fallen over the bow, when the beast had brought Maisie up from the crimson sea, a huge spike of sound had been caught on the sonobuoys. It'd spiked again when I'd attacked Don.

I listened to the recording in my cabin. It was a single word, repeated over and over by my daughter and my wife: MORE.

I knew what I had to do.

MORE.

If you could see your family again, the family you

thought you'd lost forever, is there anything you wouldn't sacrifice?

Is there *anyone* you wouldn't sacrifice?

March 16th

Maisie's hand had a way of appearing in mine. It did again this morning.

I lay on my bunk, eyes closed, the hum buzzing in my ears, whispering a promise almost fulfilled. I'd woken from a dream of us holidaying on our yacht. I could hear Julia in the galley, singing while she prepared lunch. In the dream, I sat on the main deck looking out at the ocean. A perfectly calm cerulean sea, with a cloudless sky above. I could feel the sun's warmth on my face. A small hand slipped into mine. I closed my fingers around it.

Held it tight.

Held on.

Please don't go again.

The hand followed me out of my dream.

I didn't dare open my eyes for fear that Maisie wouldn't be there. I felt the hand tugging, urging me to get up. It was time.

After Don, I killed the photographer. I lured him up onto the main deck, jumped him, and choked him out with his camera strap. I then threw him into the ocean with sandbags tied to his legs. Each time another member of the crew died, the creature rose higher and Julia and Maisie called to me more clearly.

MORE.

Conrad was next. I smashed his skull with an oxygen tank and then tipped him over the bow. After I was done, I found a trail of small wet footprints leading along the deck. They ended at the railing where Maisie had returned to the sea. With each death my family drew closer.

I knocked out Geoff and Kyle with a large dose of sedative from our medical supplies, emptied into their water rations. I tied Geoff's hands above his head and used rigging rope to drag him along behind the boat as I navigated the strait. I heard him screaming as the beast rose to consume him.

A new recording was waiting for me when I descended into the lab.

SOON, Julia promised.

SOON, Maisie echoed.

That just left Kyle.

Maisie tugged at my hand, pulling me out of bed. I kept my eyes closed as she led me through the ship and up onto the deck. I could hear Kyle struggling against his bindings. Pleading through the gag I'd fastened over his mouth.

"Open your eyes, Daddy."

"But…"

"It's okay, Daddy."

I opened my eyes.

She was gone. Kyle was lying, bound, at my feet. Like Geoff, his hands had been tied above his head. I didn't remember doing that. The rope from his arms stretched to the winch used to lower the ROV. His legs had been tied to the ROV itself. Had Julia done this?

Kyle thrashed against his bindings.

We'd left the strait in the early hours of the morning, and were heading further into the open ocean. I'd spotted a burning boat in the distance the night before. I wondered if a loved one's call had led them here. More boats had gathered overnight. More grieving souls? More blood for the beast?

MORE.

I released the ROV and watched as it began to lower towards the water. Kyle's ropes snapped taut. He was lifted off of the deck as the ROV dropped into the sea. The deeper it descended, the tighter his bindings became. He wailed through his gag; his body was stretched until there was the awful sound of limbs popping from their sockets. Moments later, his skin began to tear. Kyle came apart with a wet rip. His lower body sank with the ROV, his organs uncoiling into the ocean behind it.

I wandered up to the bow to wait.

I could see more boats in the distance now, and ahead the water had begun to bubble and churn. It was rising.

Soon a thousand eyes would breach the surface.

Soon Julia and my Maisie would return.

I sat on the deck and looked down at my bloodstained, empty hands.

THE LAST DIVE

BY CATARINA PRATA

The problem with being left for dead was that it put things into perspective.

From the beginning, the dive was reckless. We were too eager, too hasty, thinking ourselves the very best. We trained, studied and prepared repeatedly, for days turned weeks and months. Months turned to years of diving. But, as always, we screwed up the ending. And in what I thought would be my final hours, time stretched long enough that it allowed me to see the main problem with this insanc attcmpt.

We were stupid. Or, rather, Adam was insane, and I was an idiot for going down with him, just because of the fucking buddy rule. Drilled into us from the start, every single trainer we had told us that diving was not a solo sport. The rule was simple: stick with your buddy. And that meant everything, from sharing the dive plan to cross-checking the equipment, but, especially, keeping an eye on each other. Which he certainly forgot to do once I told him something was wrong, at the two hundred metres mark. Just a little left to go to break the Guinness World Record. To fulfil his dream of being amazing, and finally stop doing such risky dives. That was why I thought it was worth it: because we could finally stop.

But then my light started to flicker, and I panicked, the water transforming from deep dark blue into nothingness, the only focus of light Adam's, and my surroundings closing in. It is strange how you can feel claustrophobic on the open ocean, but in that first flicker of light, a feeble moment, everything that could go wrong came crashing down on me: my throat blocked, my breath quickened, swirling around searching for him, *losing oxygen faster*.

And then it was back. Just like the snap of a finger, I could see in front of me again and so I swam to Adam, signalling that my equipment wasn't right. We had to go up. It would take too long still to ascend, and I couldn't risk it.

And that was when I first saw it. The big cold blue light, just some metres below us. And Adam saw it too. He mimicked going down to check and did not wait for my compliance, turning and swimming farther away. My light flickered again, and the fear set in.

I moved with as much speed as I could, following his light, afraid that if I stood my ground the darkness would devour me. I could feel it. The crushing strength and impossible darkness, slowly engulfing me, reaching out with dark claws, invisible monsters all around me ready to strike. The silence, once so welcome, was intimidating, and my head turned of its own accord, left to right, right to left, in search of something, anything, that could come for me. For us. Following the light, getting to the bottom of what it was. Then getting the hell out. This was dangerous. This was reckless. This was not how we were taught at all, and he knew it; why was he doing this, why was he going down, what about what he promised, *wasn't this the last time, damn it?!*

I chastised myself, going further into the deep. I was a diver, not a scared child. All my life had been for this. The Mariana, the World Record. So that Adam could be happy.

And then we'll have done everything together, don't you see?

So that we could have a life beyond the deep sea.

When we get back, maybe we can embark on another type of adventure, since we did it all, already.

So that we could be a family.

Of course, we will be together! You're my diving buddy, right? And you know the rules, babe. You never dive without a diving buddy!

So that we could—

Come back to bed, Celia. You overthink things way too much. We are happy, aren't we?

Stop panicking. Stop. You are fine. Adam is right there; nothing is going to happen to you. Remember the rules, Celia. Keep breathing, or you will have bigger problems than a flickering light. Lung overexpansion injuries are no joke.

I breathed gradually and tried to focus on the shimmering blue light. It was not another diver, that I knew. No matter what type of equipment was used, the same shade of beige light helped identify divers. Could it be a predator? We had studied some creatures, but most of them were harmless for humans. Too small to want a piece of us, or too used to other diets altogether. Still, some of them had nasty teeth, and tearing our suits, *or something worse*, was not the best idea. I quickened the pace and got to Adam's side. He turned to look at me but averted his gaze once the blue light stopped. I had to remind myself not to hold my breath in anticipation. Adam moved slowly and surely but I intercepted him. We couldn't risk touching that thing until we knew more about it.

My light flickered again. I kept breathing, bathed by both Adam's and the blue light. And then, my back to him, I advanced on the light.

I was close when it went out, stopping me dead in my tracks, because I could feel it again. Something was wrong. We had dived fifty metres more searching for it, and now it was out. Like it had a purpose. Like it had been luring us all along. *Oh, no.*

Adam was still where I had left him. I turned to warn him and that was the moment my light failed. This time it wasn't just a glitch, but a full minute. I counted the seconds, whilst trying to get closer to Adam, to get away from that bad feeling. Everything had felt wrong with this from the beginning, and now my light was off.

And then it turned on again.

And I saw it.

Right in front of me.

My scream was muffled by the equipment, as I kicked the fins and backed away as fast as I could

Get Adam, get away; do not ascend, you are going too fast; it's a monster, it's a real sea monster; keep breathing steady, your oxygen will drop; IT'S A FUCKING MONSTER RUN AWAY, SWIM, DO IT NOW!

It was faster. I felt its teeth sink, razor sharp and excruciating. A scream that was never heard, raging inside my head. My light flickered and I was terrified to see a shape in the darkness, blacker than black, with red and blue lights covering all its body, head to tail. A dark parody of a Christmas tree, pulling back, leaving my leg with a swift silent movement. As the light came back, it had vanished and I could see a problem, spreading into the thick water, almost as dark as the ocean in the deep. Blood.

My suit was ripped. And my left leg was a mess of deep crimson and pain. It still moved when I tried to swim, but the pain reverberated through me in waves, the cold water penetrating my skin, the pressure amounting on the injury. Feeling like it could burst.

No, no, no, no, no, no.

That was the moment I turned to signal Adam, and found he was not there. My first thought, *IT GOT HIM,* quickly pushed away when I saw a distant movement upwards, and a light that was further away from me than previously expected. I refocused my eyes through tears of agonizing pain and saw him, then. Adam was ascending, as fast as he could without endangering his lungs. Leaving me behind.

You are overthinking things way too much.

We're happy, aren't we?

My light went out.

In the complete and soundless darkness that enveloped me, my leg throbbing, my thoughts cramming into me, wordless screams and

no, no, no, no, no, no

the pain and

oh, no, please, no

darkness

somebody

pain

ADAM!

loneliness

It hurts… someone, please, make it stop

light.

The light was on again.

This dive was a mess since step one. Only basic steps considered, not a big enough number of teammates, a risky practice for an even riskier dive. And I had accepted it. I hadn't even…

My breathing stopped.

You must keep breathing steady, Celia. Different breathing rhythms can and will endanger your lungs in the long term. Do you hear me?

The equipment. He picked it up. He packed it. He...

Babe I checked, it's fine, can we keep going now?

He…

He didn't, Celia.

I whimpered, pushing myself up for a short moment. My leg refused to move as it should, but I still had my fins and the rest of the equipment. I could ascend by myself. I would because

Where is it?

the creature of the depths was nowhere to be seen. And if it had tasted my blood and vanished, then maybe it did not cat human flesh. Maybe it felt attacked, maybe…

Maybe it went to get others.

I forced my leg harder, helping the movement with my arms, the sudden fear overwhelming the senses, making it harder to time my breathing, to focus, to see or hear anything at all except that stupid little scream—

Wait... what?

My wrist was screaming. Audibly. The drive computer was flashing, oxygen levels wild. At this breathing rate, I wouldn't have enough to ascend.

Panic overflowing, trying to calm my thoughts

I am going to die down here, nobody will ever find me, I can't make it, I can't

I pushed myself again, gritting my teeth and regulating my breath as my left leg waved blow me. My arms were moving the quickest, legs only helping, dive computer screaming, following a path that could go anywhere, slowly but surely ascending, imagining the sun, a boat, the shore, anything, everything. I could make it, I had to, was a diver in my soul and not just because of Adam, was not afraid, was not, I could do it, I would be fine, hell I can go faster, better to risk going to the hospital than stay here a moment longer, why are you breathing like that again STOP DOING THAT BE CALM YOU STUPID FUCKING CHILD!

The light went out again and I stopped. One minute passed and I kept counting. Two minutes. Three. My left leg. I couldn't feel it anymore. That wasn't necessarily bad, was it? I mean, it could be the effect of being in the water, or maybe it hadn't been that deep maybe everything was just out of control and why does it feel like there is something in the dark, why can't I hear anything, why, why, WHY?

Cold blue light. My heart skipped a beat. Below me, a single blue light was shimmering. Waves of terror reached inside my chest and pulled, my leg starting to pulsate, like it was connected to the creature, and knew it was coming. The blue light moved, as if searching, starting to approach. It was the last push I needed to gather my resolve and try again, metres flashing up, and up, faster than normal. I was not about to survive this and collapse my lungs, no way, no, it was going to work; I just had to breathe, keep breathing, you got this.

The blue light faded as I reached two hundred metres and relief settled in, thoughts of how stupid I had been for not pulling up, how I was scared for nothing, things were going to work out, this was life at the deep blue, and I just had to focus on the less threatening beautiful species of the dark and keep swimming as if…

Wait.

What other beautiful species? Where was the ocean life, apart from what we'd seen those first few dozen metres? As I felt my leg go numb again, and duplicated my efforts, realisation started to set in, bathing me in cold sweat. I was thankful my light had not gone out again, or I would be drowning in horror. In fact, now that I tried to focus through the blue light, the ocean didn't look so—

Blue light. Cold. Blue. Light.

The realization hit me all at once, paralysing me. It was not my light that I was using as means to reach the surface. That light had turned off a long time ago. Most importantly, my light was not cold blue, and I had been blindly following it, lost in thought, foolish in the face of panic. I knew this light. I thought I had escaped from it.

In front of me, there was an entrance to a secluded cave, and I saw another cold blue light shimmering in the darkness, finally understanding. There were no more creatures around because I had steered into their territory. As the light behind me seemed to grow, dread made me turn around. I counted at least fourteen. Fourteen blue lights, jointed as one big blue sun shining in the Mariana deep, glowing like the salvation I would never know, stuck within the gigantic darkness of the ocean. My alarm beeped again, like a piercing scream in the silence, warning of the oxygen slowly evading the tank. As one, the lights turned off, and I could sense them then, surrounding me, their fins in the darkness, their eyes and minds focused as one, my blood a trail they followed in search for more. Carnivore fish from the depths, like a very real B-rated movie. I looked in each direction, blind and at their mercy, spun mindlessly in the water, thinking I could spend all my oxygen, maybe suffocate before they all attacked, maybe take of my regulator and just drown, numbness and water taking me instead of pain and teeth.

Something touched me and I moved away reflexively, whimpering in my mind. Around me, the

Christmas red and the cold blue formed together, but my eyes were fixed on an object filled with bite marks, descending into the unknown of the trench, rolling through the current. As the lights caught it, the black spaces where his eyes used to be fixated on mine and all the bite marks in the world couldn't keep me from noticing who that head belonged to.

As they came for me in the darkness, swift lights moving through, ripping into the oxygen tanks—my legs, my arms, face, neck, the regulator falling from my mouth, the creatures destroying every living cell on my body, the water pressure burning my insides—the first and only thing I heard rippling through the trench was a poignant scream of visceral pain.

PRESSURE DIFFERENTIALS

BY HANNAH HULBERT

I settle down into my bunk and close my eyes as the crew lock us into the house. Their shouts and laughter are lost in the thud and clang of the circular door as they seal the airlock from the outside. And even when they're done, we're still surrounded by the hum and whirr of machinery and clunking, grinding metal equipment. The rest of the dive team creak and groan all around me as they try to get comfortable in their bunks.

"*You all okay in there, Tara?*" a fuzzy voice calls through the intercom.

I lift the handset to my face and hold down the button to transmit.

"Yeah, ready when you are," I reply.

"*Roger that. Beginning blowdown.*"

And then the noise starts up in earnest as the pressuriser switches on.

Going into sat is more tedious and uncomfortable than anything else. Tedious as we pass the time in this tin can, waiting for the saturation chamber to reach the same pressure we'll be under when we're down on the seabed. Uncomfortable as our bodies adjust to the pressure and the heliox they pump inside for us to breathe. I fiddle with the neck of my shirt as the heat and humidity begin to rise. My muscles ache already and I can hear the others shifting to click their stiffening joints.

Ray and Mason chat excitedly in hushed tones on the bunks below me and I smile at their childlike excitement, like kids who can't sleep on Christmas Eve. I'm pleased to be teamed up with them again. I know they look forward to the novelty of sat after life onshore; the contrast between the busyness of the work and the quiet mystery of the seabed. I doubt they'd be so enthusiastic if this was all they had, though. They have families waiting for them and their fat paycheques to come home to in a month. They're not like me.

In the bottom bunks on the other side of the miniscule sleeping compartment are the two old hands, Harry and Leon (who is serving as our medic). They've already inserted their headphones and got cracking on the hours of TV downloaded on their pressure-resistant tablets. Our paths have crossed before and they always seemed affable enough—that's one of the top qualities a saturation diver needs. They've been a lot more reserved than usual, though, and I wonder whether the idea of serving under a woman has ruffled their feathers. But they haven't caused any trouble. A few days in close quarters should help us acclimatise to each other. I've never been in a team that didn't stabilize after a day or two in sat.

I turn my head so that I'm looking straight across at the sixth member. He's laid on his back, staring up at the curved, rivet-studded ceiling, wringing his hands and grinding his teeth. The lad's on his first full mission. He's named Jonah, which gave everyone a good laugh all those miles and days and universes ago when we first met before boarding the *Clara-May*.

"Hey, kid," I squeak. My voice already sounds like that of a cartoon chipmunk.

His head jerks to face me. His eyes are wide and his smooth face is drawn and pale.

"You alright?"

He nods but doesn't say anything, rubbing his cheek against the pillow.

He was so bright and vibrant yesterday evening, full of lusty anecdotes, making himself right at home on the team. He even beat me at arm wrestling, which none of the others have managed. But today he's shrivelled to a shadow of his former self. I guess that even five years' experience in commercial diving and the sat qualification course can't fully prepare you for your first real dive.

He's right; there's something different about being out on the open sea. Something surreal about being cooped up in a metal tube, knowing there's nothing but open skies above that you can't see and cold, dark water below. It's weird being surrounded by a shipful of people whose only job is to make sure you stay alive, but you can't see any of them. It gets difficult to remember where you are, and every now and then there's a flash of confusion that you're in the wrong place at the wrong time. It's unsettling, knowing that it will take days of decompression to safely return to the world we're just a layer of metal away from.

But these are all things we knew we'd have to handle when we signed up for the job. The world's made up of three types of people: sat divers who learn to tune them out; sat divers who lean into them and learn to love it; and people who aren't sat divers.

I give Jonah a grin of reassurance, but it doesn't seem to help much. I guess by the end of this job he'll know for sure which kind of person he is.

The bell comes to a stop with a dull *thunk* when we reach the bottom. I've assigned Mason as bellman, which he shrugged at. I'm having the hardest time reading the man, but at least if he's got a problem with me he's keeping it to himself.

Mason hauls the hatch open and I step inside first. The water laps around my knees, cold and dark and enticing. Then he lowers the massive metal hat over my head. The weight on my shoulders is tremendous and instantly muffles all sound, until that little voice pipes up in my ear.

"*Testing comms. Do you read me, Tara?*" it says.

"I read you," I answer in my hilariously high-pitched voice. The surface team uses a descrambler to understand us, but we just have to get used to it on our end.

Mason and Jonah fasten the hat onto the brand-new suit and triple check the umbilicals. I glance up at the kid and am flooded with doubt. He looks awful.

"All okay, Jonah?" I ask over the comm.

"Yeah, I'll be fine," he says, but even that squeaky voice can't mask his nerves.

I had hoped getting out of the house would help him relax a bit. Everyone finds it tight, utilitarian and uncomfortable, because that's exactly what it is. But you hardly even notice after you get back from a shift at the bottom. All you want to do is refuel and sleep.

It's being on the bottom that makes the job worth putting up with that. It's always different down there: a million secret worlds no one has ever seen before. I've been looking forward to getting back down ever since my last mission. Nothing on earth can compare.

Mason and the surface crew both run their tests and then give me the all-clear. Mason can get Jonah's hat on by himself and then he'll join me. I drop down through the hatch, water swallowing me up as I descend into the darkness.

I fall rather than climb down, dragged by my weighted boots. When I land silently on the seabed, they raise a cloud of sediment. I flick my lights on, but they only illuminate the particles drifting around me and I can't see any further than my own outstretched arm. I stick next to the bell, waiting for Jonah to drop down after me. The dirt settles and I take these moments of solitude to really soak it all in. The utter black. The isolation. The sheer otherness of the place.

Hot water floods my suit, keeping my body from freezing at this extreme depth. This new oilwell we're assigned to maintain is at a depth of 585 metres of seawater—the deepest well-mouth so far. Mason promised his kids he'll be in the Guinness book of World Records. I guess Venture Petroleum's running out of places to drill and been forced to look further down. That's okay with me though. These new suits were specially designed to deal with the higher pressure. The job is the same at 300 MSW as it is here. The main difference is two extra days of decompression, but the pay will take the edge off of that.

There's chatter over the comm, a mixture of the dull baritone of the surface operator and the high-pitched squeals of Mason and Jonah. Then Jonah himself appears, sinking down beside me on clouds of sediment and rays of torch light. His face is lit inside the window of his hat and he looks like he's going to be sick. I'm seriously questioning my decision to make him press on through.

We need to be able to trust one another on a job like this. Much as I love the solitude, it's not safe to work alone. But then I think of calling the shift to a halt before we even get started. I imagine how furious the rest of the team and the crew of the *Clara-May* and the big bosses at the top would be. I consider swapping Jonah in as bellman. But the thought of entrusting my life to his trembling hands, alone in a metal sphere at the bottom of the sea, fills me with an unfamiliar dread. So instead I give him a thumbs up and lead him in the direction of the pipeline.

It's not just the visibility that makes walking difficult. Our boots sink into the thick layer of silt and the water is a translucent barrier we must constantly force our way through. I put my foot down and something shifts underneath it, almost sending me sprawling. Something flashes past through the drifts of grit—some sort of eel, I think. I laugh like a villainous woodland creature and turn back to check on Jonah.

His eyes are wide and dart about frantically. No

matter how I reassure him, he still looks ready to run. But where would he run to down here? There's only the bell, and that only leads back to the house. I tell myself that once we get to work it'll take his mind off things and lead him on again. I know that always works for me. A couple of hours of manual labour in the most serene place on this blue planet and everything else just drifts away.

I think it's something to do with the temperature of the water circulating inside the suits. It comes in hot, but after a few minutes it's cooled to body temperature, making it difficult to tell where I end and the water begins. The poor visibility and constant white noise of the water as we press through it add to the effect. 'Sensory deprivation,' they call it. Every now and then it can play tricks on you. Which is just one of the many reasons we never work solo.

The massive bulk of the pipeline looms through the darkness ahead. And then a beam of light falls over us, casting our long shadows onto the grimy exterior. The Remote Operated Vehicle has turned up at the same time as us. The ROV operators think they're the real stars of the show, but there's no way they could do the job without us. You can't beat a pair of human hands.

We work mostly in silence. It takes all our concentration to get such an arduous job done in such a hostile environment. I switch off my light and work by touch alone. The lights only really illuminate the billows of sediment anyway. But every time I glance over at Jonah, he's still got his light on.

Time loses all meaning. The surface team keep us apprised of how long we have on the clock, as well as supplying our heliox and hot water and electricity. But they're so far away, so alien, it's like they're in another world. We are separated by hundreds of metres of sea water and days of decompression. They're up there in the realm of light and open skies while we're down here, wrapped in water and darkness.

At one point I turn to peer into the open water, away from Jonah and the pipe and the ROV. Away from these last strains of humanity. It's like there's something out there, calling to me. Calling me to come find it. Or them. I can almost make out the sound of the sing-song voice against the whispering of the water. I can almost make out the shape of it through the clouds and the black. Something almost human. Something with arms outstretched, offering me the embrace I've been longing for. But then a voice through the comm jerks me out of my private world and I can't see anything at all. I imagined the whole thing.

"How're you doing, Jonah?" I ask.

"Okay," he says. His voice is bland and steady. He's got quite a bit done and he seems to have settled down. I guess he's just staying focused on the job so I abandon any attempt at chit-chat. He looks over, into that deep nothingness where I was looking just a moment ago, as though he can see something there too. I'm sure it's nothing but coincidence. Of course there's nothing there. I let the music of the sea fill my ears—that throb and roar of pressure battering against our synthetic shells, cocooning us in sound.

I had thought that being down on the bottom yesterday helped Jonah get used to this gig. I asked him when we were back in the house how he found it and he told me it was fine – hard work but straightforward once he'd found his rhythm. But he's been just as quiet and nervous as he was before, maybe even more so. And he was tossing and turning enough in his bunk while we were scheduled to sleep that he woke me up, which is almost impossible.

So I took him to one side while Ray, Harry and Leon were still out on their shift and Mason was asleep and asked him straight up if he'd rather decompress early. We both looked, reflexively, at the emergency decompression chamber's closed hatch. We both knew how claustrophobic it gets in there. And how isolated someone would be, decompressing while the rest of the team goes on with the job on the other side of the door. How painful it would be to exist at pressures too disparate to mingle. I wasn't surprised when he declined.

"What about acting as bellman today, then?" I offered.

"No," he said, without pausing to consider, as though he had anticipated my suggestion and already reached his conclusion before I even asked. There was not a shred of doubt in his voice, and I have to admit I was glad. The thought of the kid being responsible for keeping me alive is not a comforting one.

And so it's just the two of us down here again today. If it can be called day, in this place without sunlight. Mason admitted he actually prefers bell duty, so that works out best for everyone. I would have done the job, but I'm not sure how well Mason would look out for Jonah; he's a bit of a practical joker. And I'd rather not miss an opportunity to go out. Being here at the bottom of the North Sea isn't everyone's idea of a treat but it absolutely is for me.

Jonah has his light on again and I have no idea how he manages to get any work done with that grubby water lit up between him and the pipe. The ROV is doing all the heavy lifting. But the operators rely more on us for directions and help with the fiddly details than we do on their strong robot arms. You can say what you like about humans, but I wouldn't swap my analogue body for any enhancements.

As I rummage in my tool belt, fumbling for the right wrench, I hear that melodious voice again. I lift my eyes and cast them about the deep emptiness. Only, it's not empty. It's full to bursting, every millimetre crammed full of water. And there's something else out there too, I'm sure there is. Everything is clouded and grainy outside the tiny window in the front of my hat, but I'm sure I can see someone out there. Someone reaching for me, longing to welcome me. I belong here. I've always known I belong here. And I belong with *them*, whoever they might be.

There's a shrill screech over the comm.

"Jonah!" I cry, turning back to where he was a moment ago.

He's gone.

I look around for his light but there's just the ROV blazing in the dark. I switch my own light on but that only makes things worse.

Calling for him won't help – through the comm everyone sounds the same distance away, and I'm sure he won't be able to direct me to wherever he's got to.

"Mason? Surface unit? Do you have eyes on Jonah?"

"*His readings are normal and his camera's just showing the same murky darkness as yours. I've tried asking him where he's going but he isn't responding.*"

"Do you know which way he went?"

"*His umbilical's right behind you. He's headed away from the bell.*"

"Thanks."

I grope around in the darkness until I find the bundle of tubes and wires that connects Jonah to the bell and then to the world above us. It's a thick tangle but it strikes me that the strand that connects him—and me—to the rest of humanity is incredibly small and precarious. In comparison to the breadth of the ocean, it barely exists at all. I run my hand along it as I clomp awkwardly through the silt of the seabed, struggling against the wall of thick water. Towards that spot where I thought I saw something moving just before the scream.

There's definitely something moving there now. And though my mind is a carousel of imagined wonders my pulse stays oddly steady. Perhaps it's that sensory deprivation, lulling me into a false sense of calm. I trace my numb fingers along the length of Jonah's umbilical which, too, is unnaturally still.

And then I see why.

There's a massive chunk of rusted metal ahead. It looks like a piece of machinery that dropped from a ship and sank to the bottom, decades ago. The umbilical has snagged on the jagged edge. And now I can see a light whirling and strobing through the murk ahead.

"Jonah!"

The motion stops. I round the metal debris and there he is, struggling frantically. I can see his mouth moving inside his hat but I can't hear a thing. Maybe the comm line was damaged when his umbilical got caught?

"Jonah, if you can hear me, give me a wave."

He waves with both hands like a sailor lost at sea,

flagging down a rescue chopper.

"It's okay, I'll sort you out, just stop tugging. Tara to crew—I've got him. Umbilical caught on some debris but otherwise seems fine. Stand by."

I go slowly, talking each step through with the rest of the team as they monitor Jonah's readings for any clues that his equipment has been damaged. Other than his transmitter, it's all intact, and I extract him safely from that hunk of savage edges.

It's tough getting him to follow me back. He keeps looking over his shoulder, into the darkness as it reclaims the ground we had desecrated with our light only a moment before. We pass the ROV with its dead eyes. We follow our umbilicals, those tethers that bind us to the rest of humanity. And climb back into the bell, where Mason is waiting for us.

Jonah is trembling as he ascends the rungs. I make him go first, for fear that he may not go at all if he doesn't have me chivvying him from behind. But also, I'm finding it hard to drag myself away. I can feel the deep calling me back, too. I'm brimming with guilt at forcing Jonah back into the house he dreads returning to, because I, too, share that dread.

———

I almost insisted Jonah head straight for the emergency decompression chamber when we got back to the house.

Of course Leon, Harry and Ray had heard all about what had happened by then, even though we were returning early, halfway through their sleep shift. When we stepped out of the wet room the three of them were all waiting, grim-faced, to greet us. And Mason took up his position between Harry and Ray, as if picking a side.

The house is always pressurised, until the job is over and we go through the days of decompression in order to re-enter the world. But this is different. It's like something heavy is weighing on us all, constantly, crushing our spirits.

Jonah refused to go into the chamber. The others all started yelling at him. What does he expect the rest of us to do about this mess, now that we're a man down but still stuck with that man using up our space and heliox? It would've been a right laugh, all of these big men squealing like little piggies in their stupid voices, if it hadn't been so serious. Dive teams never argue in sat. We need to trust each other, to tolerate each other's idiosyncrasies. It's the only way to endure a month living in such tight quarters and working in such a harsh environment. I've never seen a team act like this. It's like something's gotten into them. Like Jonah's affecting them all. He's like a ghost that refuses to be exorcised, dragging us all down to a watery grave with him.

Jonah insisted the umbilical incident was just a mistake he won't make again, and that it hasn't affected his ability to work. He said he got disoriented and thought he was heading back to the bell for lunch. He didn't know how he ended up taking the wrong direction at the wrong time, using the wrong protocol by going alone without telling anyone first. The others frowned incredulously as he told us this, and I didn't blame them. His words rang with falsehood. But the only way of dealing with that was to feign belief or call him a liar to his face, and we hadn't devolved to barbarism quite that far yet.

I knew there was no way Mason or any of the others would trust him as bellman after what had happened, though. And there was no way I'd trust any of them to keep an eye on Jonah and get the job done at the bottom. No, I was the only one I could trust on the bottom with the kid. And so I had been backed into picking a side too. Which is how I ended up working next to Jonah maintaining the pipe under the watchful, inanimate eye of the ROV again today.

We're both sluggish and dull today, and not just because of our wariness, lest we have a repeat of yesterday's events. Neither of us slept well last night. Jonah kept me up with his restlessness, but I doubt I would've slept anyway. Every time I closed my eyes I saw that figure shifting in the darkness, reaching out to me. That haunting voice called to me, a cadence somewhere between speech and singing.

I can hear it calling now. There's a flicker of motion

in the black depths of the ocean outside our pool of obnoxious light. I take a glance at Jonah. He's looking in the same direction.

"You saw that too?" I ask.

He nods. We've tested the comms and they're working fine. He's choosing not to speak. As though his stupid, high-pitched voice will sully the beauty of the moment.

And he's right. It is beautiful. The voices of the surface crew and Mason are bombarding me as I set down my tools and follow the song, but I tune them out. The further I get from the bell, the easier it becomes.

"*Tara!*" someone is screaming into my ear. "*Your umbilical won't stretch! Come back!*" But whoever it is yelling these instructions is irrelevant. They're miles away, in another existence. The pressures weighing on us are so utterly different, we could never reconcile. Jonah is walking alongside me now, as though reassuring me that ignoring the other voices is the correct choice. The only real option.

But a moment later I'm pulled to a halt. The umbilical has reached its full capacity. Jonah reaches round to the back of his hat and tugs at his, but it's clamped on quite securely. We're both forced to stop, after having come so close. I can see that figure just out of reach, inviting us home. And how I long to go home.

Not home to that blinding, empty expanse of sky. Not into that metal coffin filled with fake air. Not that place they call a house, sealed in with those people who are not family or even friends. Jonah and I don't belong there. We never belonged there. I contemplate returning to the house and going through days of decompression again, all to emerge into a world I never wanted to be a part of in the first place. The notion makes me nauseous.

The figure in the dark must have noticed that we are restrained, because it is approaching us now. As it comes closer, I realise that it is not humanoid, as I had first imagined. It is far more beautiful: a small, suspended body with four slender, equal-length limbs trailing beneath. And as it draws nearer I can see that there are more limbs reaching ahead, towards me. Longing to embrace me.

The sound I had been ignoring through the comm grabs my attention again. It's the sound of Jonah, gasping. I turn to him with a smile on my face and am astonished to see his mouth hanging open in terror through the brightly lit window of his hat. What could he have seen to horrify him so utterly that it overrode the wonder our visitor has inspired?

Jonah turns and begins to retreat back towards the bell, stirring silt all around him as he does. The visitor (or are we the visitors, and this our host?) glides serenely through the space before me, to greet me.

Its song fills my heart; my life; my world. Its beauty is devastating. Tears run down my cheeks, but I cannot brush them away. The hat covers my face still, preventing me. Separating me from my beloved. Their limbs extend and enfold me in ecstasy. Their body wafts like an angel's wings. They press in closer, promising to free me from this synthetic husk. To bless me with a kiss.

I lift my face to receive it. And know that I am where I belong.

THE MANY GHOSTS OF THE DEEP

BY CRAIG WALLWORK

It begins with the sound of the world yawning. Or the sky being ripped in two. Everyone hears it. Everyone is united in that moment and gripped by the same expression of fear. The cabin shakes. Metal groans. All at once the plane drops and you recall as a child riding a roller-coaster, and a vertical drop of fifty feet that turns your stomach into a washing machine drum on spin. A chorus of screams. A salvo of creaks and moans from the wings, and beside you your daughter drops her colouring book and says, “Mommy?” That’s when you know, right then, that a lover will never kiss her. Right at that moment, you know she will never become a woman.

A crackle, a pop, and hiss. An educated voice squeezes through a set of tiny speakers in the walls.

"This is captain Dowd. As you're aware, we're experiencing difficulties with the plane and we're going to attempt an emergency landing on the sea in approximately three minutes. We don't have much control, so this will be a crash landing…"

Worried voices exchange questions. There are people already calling out to God, but God is a man sat in a cockpit fighting for control over a damaged plane. God is human and preparing for death.

You feel the person behind you rummaging in the chair's backrest for that laminated sheet showing cartoon survivors on the emergency slide with a relaxed expression. And you know that in three minutes the reality is going to be anything but that.

Crack. Hiss. Captain Dowd clears his throat.

"This is going to be worse than anything you've ever been through before. Prepare yourself, and those with children, give them a hug."

Your daughter's eyes are mirrors reflecting your face, a face bent and twisted with worry. Nothing matters but her safety. You say everything is going to be okay, because saving a child from the fact the plane is a glass bottle landing on a sheet of concrete, and everyone inside will soon be crushed, or drown to death, is what a parent must do. But your face betrays all this, and your sweet little daughter, the one who only an hour ago asked if she will see angels when the plane passes through the clouds, grabs your hand, and weeps. And there's nothing left but to join her.

"We will do everything we can in our power to land this plane safely, but we need your cooperation. Please brace yourself, and whatever happens in the next couple of minutes, I wish you all luck."

The hiss from the speakers dies. The one engine working roars like a lion outside the window.

Rewind five hours. Liverpool's John Lennon airport. You're on the phone to your husband, giving the times when Flight 876 will land at Belfast. You tell him you've missed him, and that you're sorry for leaving on bad terms. He says it doesn't matter. That we shouldn't argue about money. Everything will work out. And you say that your parents are going to help, just for the short term, until he's found a job. But all he wants right now is you back home in Bangor. All he wants is to hear his daughter's voice. So, you pass the phone to her, and like any child of five years, she talks about all the things she did and how Nanna and Granddad let her ride a pony, and how much candyfloss she ate at the park, and the new teddy she called Floppy Dog. And you hear your husband of ten years on the other end ask Floppy Dog to look after the only two people in the world he loves. But Floppy Dog failed.

The plane tilts and through the window you see a vast expanse of water stretching out toward the horizon. The sun throws a handful of diamonds on the surface and you're part in awe of its beauty, and part wondering how far down below the water the light will reach. There are noises now, like animals caught in traps, or the song of ghosts on windy moors. You hear atonements for transgressions, confessions, and hopelessness. You hear words tendered to console. But you are a whisper. You are the gentle voice in your daughter's ear that tells her she is loved and will always be loved. You are the one she will remember, the one person who knows she is the most beautiful thing in the world.

There are shouts from the front of the plane from the staff. It is the one word that chills you more than any other.

"BRACE! BRACE! BRACE!"

You lower your daughter's head, take your arm, and draw her close. She is partly over your lap and you're sheltering her with your body. Through the window you see the ocean coming into view. The diamonds have faded away, but the surface is calm, and you are thankful for these gifts. Maybe the plane won't be a glass bottle thrown against concrete. Maybe, it'll be more like a pebble skimming across water. Maybe, just maybe…

You hardly have time to register the plane hitting the water, but the echo of that bang accompanies you into the darkness.

———

You don't feel anything in the first moments. Then you realise you're not dead because death is not painful. Death is numbness and obscurity, whereas the world you are born back into is cold, bright, and filled with the screams of a hundred injured passengers. Lights blink erratically in the cabin. Above your head, masks hang down like jellyfish. The space between you and the other row of chairs has reduced, but not as much as you expected. There is still room to breathe. Eyes coated in blood now. Everything looks like photos suspended in a developing room. The warmth you feel comes from your child, and you hope it remains, that life will not leave her little body and turn it cold. You raise her head from your lap, and she is sleeping in your hands. You pray she is sleeping. Blood drips from your forehead on her pale skin, and you wipe it away like so many tears from her eyes following a graze, or in the wake of a nightmare. The air is charged with pleas, petitions, and bargaining. There is anger and rejoicing, and the plane is more a church for the redeemed and the thankful. God has done his job and brought them down safely.

Hallelujah!

Your feet turn cold as ice. There's something that feels like a bony finger pressing against your neck. It is only when you hear a man's voice yell that the water is coming in that you realise the plane is sinking. There are cracks in the walls, and jets of brine that once coated the lips of fishermen bleed in. The window beside you is divided in two. One part sky. The other water. You can see below the surface, and it is dark, and you know there is more horror awaiting you below than that which exists above. Some passengers are up on their feet, scrambling toward the emergency exits. A woman's elbow strikes you in the head. A young man pushes past another. A fight breaks out. And all the while you cradle your child, rocking her gently as you did when she was a baby.

"Fuck you!"

"Get out of my way!"

"Bitch!"

"Let the children leave first!"

"You selfish bastard!"

"My wife is dead!"

"Help me!"

The plane is no longer a church. It is the first day of Black Friday when the doors open in the department store. It is a prison during a breakout. It is Hell unleashed.

Your eyes fall to the window, which is now more water than sky. You convince yourself an angel passed by. But you realise angels don't exist in the water. Like your daughter said, they belong in the clouds. A mermaid? A porpoise? You turn to the man in the aisle with his hands gripped around the shoulders of another man, and you say, "Did you see that? In the water?" But he doesn't hear you because he's yelling that everyone is equal in the godforsaken place. But nobody is. When the shit hits the fan, or in this case, the pigeons hit the engine, everyone is out to protect themselves. You come to the understanding that charity is a placebo to make us feel better. That humility and compassion are not the currency of choice in survival. Instead, violence, anger, and selfishness are the tools that will free you.

There's an argument that is louder than any other. One man is yelling that the door will not open. You look over the headrests. Men of various sizes and strength yank at the handle, but the door won't budge. A woman uses the heel of her shoe against one window. Another man is trying to gain access to the cockpit. People act like ants following a stampede. They are erratic and without order. They are chaos in a sardine can.

"Sweetheart," you say to your sleeping daughter. "It's time to wake up. Daddy is waiting."

She remains in slumber. You place the life vest over her head. The steward said you're not supposed to blow on the small valve until you are outside of the plane. Fuck that. You inflate the vest anyway, then repeat the process again for you.

There's a thud, and the whole pane tilts to the left. Everyone standing is thrown to the floor or into the chairs beside them. Your daughter almost slips from your lap. You gather her up like old laundry, and that's when you realise the water level is up to your knee. People yell and question what the fuck had the power to move a plane. There is speculation. Conjecture. Someone says it's the water filling the fuselage, causing it to tumble. Soon, the plane will become too heavy and sink to the bottom of the Irish Sea where old trawlers sleep in decay, and the ghosts of fishermen roam the bed. This is your fate now. You and everyone else will be ghosts beyond the deep. As people scramble to their feet, there's another loud bang that rocks the plane, causing the lights to go off. Darkness moves through the cabin like the water, touching everyone and invading every space.

"What the fuck is it?"

"We're gonna die!"

"We need to get out now before we drown!"

"Look!"

There's a moment when all the wailing, the crying, the call for forgiveness and redemption, it all stops and everyone is looking to that one small window. You adjust your head, and though it hurts like hell, you see what everyone else can see. You see what cannot be possible.

"Is it a whale?" someone asks.

Outside the window is an eye the size of a beach ball staring back. In the sea's murk, the eye is the colour of a weeping wound, of pus, and earwax.

"That's too damn big to be a whale."

"Are you some fucking whale expert?"

"Hey buddy, use that tone with me and I'll…"

Metal cries out like the rusty cogs from an old torture rack. The space around you shifts, and the walls seem to be closing in. Water pisses through the seams in the panels, and you realise that whatever the fuck that thing is, it's coiling itself around the plane like a boa constrictor around a goat. Frenzy amplifies. Throats release noises no human should produce. With no way out, and the possibility that outside is worse than inside, you hope for a quick end. At least your daughter is sleeping. At least she is not witness to this nightmare. The overhead compartments burst open under the pressure of that monster squeezing the plane as easily as a child with a toothpaste tube. Bags, children's toys, laptops, and all the things we took for granted come spilling out like confetti. The water level is at waist height, so you kneel on the seat, cradling your daughter in your arms.

A voice amidst the panic turns to you, and says, "Is your daughter okay?"

It's a woman of around fifty years, blood-matted hair, and a gash on her forehead so big you see the white of her skull.

"She's sleeping," you tell her.

In her expression, you register uncertainty.

"I don't want to wake her," you say, and right then, the ceiling cracks in two. A sheet of black muscle squeezes through the gap. More screams as those nearest to the flesh of that monster fall into the cold waters. You observe the milk-white barnacles welded to the monster's blackened skin, and you are reminded of toadstools sprouting through graveyard soil. The monster's skin is smooth in other areas, but there are signs of war, of battles won where scar tissue is a medal, reminding other sea creatures not to fuck with you.

A man has retrieved a small fire extinguisher. He is beating the end against the monster's underbelly, a task akin to prodding a cotton bud against a rhino's arse.

More constriction and the walls yield. Water pours in and the only thing plugging the biggest hole in the plane is the monster. You stand now on the chair, lifting your daughter with you. Those on the aisle are treading water. There are no lights. Just cold, and the bending of metal. Beyond each small window is a vast nothingness inhabited by sea creatures, ghosts, and the soon to be wreckage of Flight 876. Sometimes you see another part of the monster as it adjusts its position around the plane. What you assume to be its fins have the same appearance of bat wings, a thin membrane of skin. What you assume to be its tail stretches out like a snake. There is no way to measure its size, but you try because you're all out of screams. You're all out of tears and goodbyes. You shiver in the cold waters and estimate it to be twice the size of the plane. Another constriction. The ceiling lowers, making the gap between the water and the monster's underbelly just over twelve inches. Your daughter is heavy in your arms, but you lift her head above the water so she can breathe. Everyone else is doing the same. They are Koi carp at feeding time. Then people who can't swim too well, or are too tired, or hurt, go under the surface, and do not return. Partners, loved ones, they try to raise them out, but it's too hard to tread water and hold another person. You hear the final gurgled screams of women, men, and children. Yes, children. Their parents call their names and go under the water to find them, and sometimes they do, but other times they never return. Probably for the best. Probably best to remain there with the children.

Twelve inches of air becomes six, and you're on your tiptoes raising your child like an offering to the Gods.

You expect the monster will tear the plane in half, and in that moment the ocean will devour the cabin. You expect that once this happens, there'll be a moment where you hold your breath and kick like hell, holding your daughter to your chest, and heading toward a light beyond the surface. And, if you've got enough air in your lungs and love in your heart, you'll pass the monster undetected. Then, maybe, the coastguard, or a rescue helicopter, will see you both bobbing like apples in the water. And before midnight, before dawn breaks, you'll be back in your husband's arms, and your daughter will sleep in her bed. This is what you expect to happen, and as the monster's muscles contract, it reduces the gap to an inch.

The cabin splits, and you say to yourself, "The ocean, or any monster in this world or the next, is not going to take my daughter from me!" And you kick like a frog dancing on a hot skillet. The vest adds buoyancy, and hope floods your heart. You're going to make it. That's what you keep telling yourself. A silver medallion of light shimmers above. That is your goal, your finish line. But even in water you hear screams and the groaning of metal. Even in water you feel the monster moving. But you don't look down. Below is the grave. Above is salvation. Muscles ache. Your ribs and ears feel the pressure of the sea, but you don't stop because if your daughter wakes, she will see a hundred bodies floating toward the bed, and that monster devouring the plane. The horror of this will change her. It will rob her of youth and happiness. So, you kick harder, and your lungs cry out for mercy, but you're a mother that will never give up, ever. And as you see the light grow brighter, and watch as the waves break the surface of the ocean, you feel against your leg something cold, something like a person's hand. The ghosts of fishermen, or the monster, you can't decide which, nor do you want to look down to make sure. There is a fleeting moment where your lungs turn hard as concrete, and you wonder if they will weigh you down, that no amount of kicking will push you to the surface. And in that fragile space of time, you kiss your daughter's cold cheek. You raise your arms so that the distance is greater between you and her. It's only inches, but it may mean she gets to breathe before you have time to. And as your hands break through the water, and the cold air is shackled to your wrists, you know you did your job. You saved her, and she will sleep not in the water forevermore, but somewhere warm surrounded by teddies and the love of her father. You are inches from taking that first gasp yourself, and you feel for the first time that everything will be okay. There is no need to worry. As your husband says, as long as you have each other, you can win the impossible battles. If you have each other, you can beat off monsters and the ghosts of old fishermen. And the smell of air is sweet as honeysuckle, and sunlight is a tonic that bloats your heart. You take all of God's gifts into your lungs and feed off life. The noise of gulls and wind is a sonnet, and you cannot, nor ever, forget how wonderful it is to be alive. In the distance, chopper blades slice up clouds. You taste the brine on your lips, and you wonder if the ocean is just the tears of the fishermen's widows. You pull your daughter close, wipe the ocean from her face. She sleeps in blissful ignorance. You get one chance to tell her you love her before you feel something graze your leg. You get one final chance to hold her before you feel something cold wrap around your ankle. The chopper blades churn the air. The seagulls cackle and holler. Bubbles rise from below, and as you look down, the colour of the water has changed from dark blue to green. You get one final chance to say to your daughter you're sorry you can't be there when she goes home, but you'll carry her love to the deep.

You feel tension in your leg, and before you can say anything else, you are watching your daughter from below, bobbing on the ocean surface. You raise your hand to touch her, but she is too far away, and with every second that passes, you are carried into darkness where bodies are suspended like angels on a Christmas tree. The flotsam of the wreckage swirls to the monster's movements, and you are united with the many ghosts of the deep.

THE END OF THE LINE

BY JACK HARDING

The rod cut through the winter's sky in a perfectly straight line as if struck across some charcoal sketch of a sunless seascape: a fine yet deliberate slash of graphite on a grey-green canvas that hung in defiance to the steady wind. The old man watched the tip of his fishing rod dreamily, and long minutes passed.

It was a bleak and bitter morning in the tenebrous depths of January, and the air had a sickly, pungent smell of salt and bad eggs that made the old man feel at home. His eyes were red-veined and heavy, morning eyes with lids of lead that cried out for the black pane of sleep. There was a warm, acidic taste in the back of his mouth, and his stomach felt as though it had been packed full of rocks. The old man was used to rising way before the crack of dawn, but that nauseating wave, that sickly morning sense still snuck up on him like an odious hangover. It was unshakeable. Immovable. Unbending. It was, in a way, much like his inert fishing rod this cold and fruitless hour.

The old man yawned and then, tilting his head to the sky, he briefly closed his eyes. He drew the cold, sulphuric essence of the ocean through his nose. The air was thin but he held it tight. Time stood still for the briefest of moments and he could practically taste the briny strands of crispy olive seaweed on his tongue and, to the old man, it tasted good. Fetid, sharp and overpowering, but good. He released the breath, then immediately drew another. The crisp blast burrowed through his crackling lungs, filling and soothing them with a touch that brought him a strange sort of comfort. In the lapping silence, he held his breath for as long as he could, and then he released it back into the wind as a pang of warped nostalgia jabbed at his mangled memory. He had been fishing these waters ever since he was ten years old but—today—he could not remember exactly how long ago that was. Frowning, he let out an exasperated sigh and returned his gaze to the tip of his rod.

——

It was somewhere between dawn and daylight, the long night reluctant to fully loosen its grip on the world as the white sun tried and failed to rear its lazy head. There was a sprawling blanket of fat, dreary clouds covering the ball in the sky today and their dirty, lead-coloured forms were reflected in the oily grey-green of the sea which ebbed and flowed in sullen waves under the persistent force of the constant wind. The sky and the sea almost seemed to melt into one, stretching out into a bare, grey horizon that mirrored the old man's mood.

He coughed, his bleary eyes tracing the translucent whisker of fishing line from the tip of his rusty pole down into the sea. He stared at the line's point of entry. Flashes of white broke the monotony of the murk as miniature waves formed then foamed, disappeared then formed again. He stared, mesmerised—almost—by the line's stillness in the half-light. His sad and narrow eyes glinted with impatience and despair, shifting aimlessly. Seeing nothing.

"Come on you bastards," he whispered, daring the line to speak. Goading it. Begging it to sing, dance, bob or shake. But it was all out of words, all out of moves. The old man sucked his yellow teeth and returned his gaze to the twisted ceiling of low clouds that swarmed across the sky like a sprawling plague of locusts, creeping sluggishly towards the island some two miles at his back.

Maybe we should head in, he thought, shuffling on the plank of frayed wood that ran the width of his tight boat. *No, we'll be fine*, he reassured himself, his eyes tracing the enormous conveyor belt of locusts as they surged overhead. They almost seemed to bear down on the little old man in his little old boat, crushing them both, forcing them deeper and deeper into the grey-green depths. It was, in many ways, a tragic scene. Like one of those old and faded postcards or paintings you saw perched on a beaten carousel in some rundown, nautical gift shop: *The Calm Before The Storm.* It was a picturesque but lonely sight. There were no other vessels in view: no tankers, no cargo ships, no yachts, trawlers or dinghies. No gulls. No nothing. Just the little old man and his little old boat and, save for the gentle slapping of the ocean waves against the wooden hull and the occasional nip of the biting wind, all was still and gentle, eerie and void of life. It was one of those days where you had to stop and wonder if the world had finally given up and stopped revolving altogether. The thought briefly patted a soft tune through the old man's head, then vanished. He sighed, his face a torn wilderness of cracks, blotches and sharply-etched lines, rough and rugged. In the grey light, his pale skin was the colour of tea with milky water, no cream. He brought a cold knuckle up to his scaly nose, wiped away a trickle of snot. He sniffed, returning the hand to the rubber handle of his rod, then he clawed at his freckled skin with a chicken-like claw that was brown with the dried blood and guts of a dozen dead ragworms. He glared up at the sea of clouds once more. They had a metallic, almost iridescent quality to them that he had never seen before—at least, not that he could remember. He frowned, dropping a fresh line down into his cloudy pool of clouded memories, fishing for the last time he saw snow. But there was nothing—no bite, no bait. His thoughts struggled vainly, almost as if they were in a dream. The old man's mind was a jumbled mess of memories and half-baked recollections; a lonely, warped world of confused half-states and demented crossovers. 'Dementia', Doctor Beaumont had called it. Or was it Doctor Pritchard? He couldn't remember. He couldn't recall the conversation in its entirety today and, besides, what did it matter? The result was the same, the outcome inevitable, his fate sealed. His senile brain was eroding by the day. Rotting like a forgotten mushroom at the back of an old refrigerator—dying. The old man sighed, returning his gaze expectantly to the tip of his rod. *Didn't it snow out here last winter?* he thought, his eyes squinting through the tiny ring at the end of his rod as if the answer lay somewhere beyond it.

"No," he croaked, wrestling with his treacherous memory as something sifted through his head: something dark; an invisible, wraith-like finger spooling around inside the chasms of his brain, hunting for the red button on his hippocampus that read 'blend'. And then it found it, and an explosion of fear and confusion went off in his mind. *No, it was back in '89, you know this. But that was last year. No it wasn't. Yes it was. Was it? It snowed last week. Where's Dad? It's empty. Go back. Dad will know. Something's out here. Dad's dead. When? '93. No. '83. Yes. Where's Margot? She's dead too. What year is it? '96. There's nothing out here. No, it's more like '66.*

The old man winced and shook his head sluggishly. He had been staring at the end of his rod for the better part of two hours now, stopping only for the odd sip of lukewarm cocoa from his flask or to gaze dully at the sky and the grim horizon. Even then he found it difficult to unhook his eyes from the prize. He would sit and trace the line up and down then up again, daring it to bend or bow or breathe or bite, but the line would not yield. Not yet.

"Magic rags, my arse," he murmured, casting his mind back to his strange encounter with the kind man in the tackle store last night. Or was it this morning? He couldn't be sure. He couldn't even remember the man's face but glimmers of the encounter rippled through his mind.

"Got some magic rags in fresh today, old boy," the young lad with the ponytail said from behind the counter, slamming a slab of newspaper down on the glass top with a smile on his face.

"Magic rags?" the old man frowned.

"That's right."

"Magic how?"

"Well," the young lad said, "this batch of worms came in from across the channel. Just off the coast of Dunkirk as it happens."

"Dunkirk?"

"That's right."

"What's so magic about them?"

"Well," he said, "I've heard that John Dory caught a conger eel the size of a bloody anaconda using these ragworms. I ain't seen any pictures mind you, but I'm sure it'll be in the papers tomorrow. Had a bloke in here earlier saying it was just off the old pier apparently. You know John Dory, right?"

The old man shook his head.

"Oh, well, doesn't matter. Anyway, these must be magic rags to snag that kind of a catch, wouldn't you say?"

"Magic Rags," the old man repeated.

"Magic Rags," the young lad behind the counter nodded.

"How much for half a pound, son?"

"For you," he said, "nothin'."

The old man frowned.

"N-nothing?" The word slithered through his cracked lips.

"That's right. They're on me, old boy. My treat."

"Oh," the old man didn't know what to say, "oh… I… I couldn't, lad."

"You can," the faceless clerk beamed, sliding the

packet of sandy worms across the top of the counter, "and you will."

"Oh, that's… that's terribly kind of you, lad."

"Just make sure you bring us back a nice fat conger or a cod, all right?" he smiled.

"I'll try," the old man returned the gesture, grabbed the package, then headed for the door.

"Magic rags, my arse," he muttered again, tearing his eyes from the tip of his frozen rod and sweeping them across the sea. "Never used to be this bloody quiet out here did it, Dad?"

There was a moment of silence, and then:

"Nope," the old man answered on his late father's behalf, his voice a low, gravel-like husk, "used to have us wily little dogfish and bream and congers and tope the size of small children. Lots of cod, bass and skate, and more rays than the bloody sun, ha."

The old man half smiled. He knew it was the exact sort of thing his dear old dad would reel off. Some days he remembered how long he'd been gone. Most days, though, he drew a blank. A part of him swore blind it could have been no less than a week or two ago that they were both out here raiding the seas like a pair of seasoned, big game fishermen. Keeping score and chewing the fat over work, women, rising fuel prices and the shitty football, the roofs of their burnt mouths throbbing with the scalding heat of pot noodles and sweet tea. They were good times. The best. Another part of the old man's mind, however, suggested he hadn't seen his dad in decades. He bowed his head and heaved another sigh, shifting his sad eyes to the small bucket of tangled, so-called 'magic rags' that were covered in a dusting of parmesan-like sand, twisting in and out of one another like clumps of bloated noodles from some intestinal nightmare. He stared into the squirming pit of rubbery flesh, legs and pincers. Hypnotised, almost, by their terrible, reddish-brown churn.

"You little bastards gonna help me out or what?" he mocked, locking eyes on an especially large worm that was a curious shade of green. It must have been at least fifteen inches long. He leant towards the bucket to get a closer look at the creature's enormous pincers. They were thick and shiny, hook-like and jet black, twitching and clicking together ceaselessly like a pair of rusty pliers.

"What about you?" The old man asked the king worm. "You fancy going down there next?"

No reply.

The old man snickered, switching his attention back to his rod. Still, there was nothing. No sign of life. He was just about to slide his hand up to the reel and reset the line when he sensed a movement. A tremor. Slight. The first touch, perhaps, of a small fish exploring the baited hook. Maybe a flounder or a garfish, a curious little rainbow bass perhaps. The old man's heart tensed. His skin felt prickly, nervous. He watched.

"Come on..." he breathed into the rising wind, his eyes bright and ravenous, glued to the tip of the whispering rod. He straightened up and shuffled forward, holding his breath, and as the air entered his lungs, he felt a sudden chill run the length of his spine, though he didn't know why.

"Take it..." he said softly to the tip of the flickering pole. The last ring on the rod was now a blur of short, intermittent vibrations, like an ailing candle flame caught in a draft. He gripped the handle tight with tenterhooks for hands.

"Go on... take it—"

And then the rod stiffened up. Froze.

There was an eerie lull in the wind as the entire area slipped into stillness, as if God—or some kind of god—had finally had enough of all the nonsense down on earth and hit pause. Everything grew quiet, silent, motionless, suspended in time and apprehension. The old man's top lip curled into a sneer. Exasperated, his eyes narrowed into puzzled slits of mulish disbelief and frustration as he glared at the lifeless rod, blinking away the cutting wind that whipped up and across his face. He cast his eyes down and stared into the grey-green depths—and then he heard it.

"*Peeeeeeeettteerrrrrrr...*"

The old man's eyes widened into cold marbles of terror.

"*Peeeeeeeeetttttteerrrrrr...*"

He tore them from the sea, twisting and turning his head around like a startled bird, the hairs of his thinning scalp rising into feathery spikes of dread.

"*Peeeeeeeeettttteerrrrrrrr...*"

The wind was calling him.

"*Peeeeeeeeettttteerrrrrrrr...*"

The wind was taunting him.

"*Peeeeeeeeettttteerrrrrrrr...*"

It was muffled yet unmistakable; the name—his name—was creeping on the air, crawling on the wind, moaning from port to starboard then back again, groaning from stern to bow then back again and his eyes frantically scanned the sky and the sea, searching for the origin of the rasping sound, clutching the spongy handle of his precious fishing rod as if it were a harpoon.

"*Peeeeeeeeettttteerrrrrrrr...*"

"Who… who's there?" he asked with fright in his voice, his eyes locked now on the old Yamaha engine just above the transom. "What… what the hell is this?"

"*Emmmpptyyyy...*"

The chilling rasp trailed off into a breathy moan and then… nothing.

Silence.

The gentle lapping of the steady waves replaced the haunting words of the wind, and the old man slowly turned his gaze back to the rod with a nervous chuckle.

"Must… must be goin' mad," he said, his face crumpled into a grey mask of incredulity and something approaching relief. "Right," he shook his head and put his sticky fingers on the plastic handle of the reel, "let's… let's try something different, shall we—"

The rod slowly bent into a severe arc, relaxed then immediately dipped towards the surface of the dark water again. Two deep, purposeful tugs curved the rod and uncreased the old man's face, plunging his stomach into a pool of bubbling excitement. He started to his feet. He slowly spread his legs shoulder-width apart, digging his heels into the stained timber of the hull. He carefully anchored the butt of the rod in the plastic cup of his fishing belt, sliding his left hand eight inches above the reel, his right hovering just below. He locked his knees, took a deep breath, and readied himself.

"…just… one… more… pull…"

Seconds felt like minutes as the old man watched, repeating the line over and over in his mind and then, as if in response to his wish, the rod slowly returned to its usual form before bowing to the sea again. It was almost as though it were breathing. The old man didn't waste a second: he clamped his right hand just below his left and jerked the rod up as hard as he could. The line jerked back with unexpected force then began to violently dart from side to side.

"Got him!" the old man said triumphantly, snapping

his right hand to the reel as his left pulled the jittering rod towards his leaning body. He lost his footing, regained it with a stubborn grunt then angled his body forward into a slight hunch. He turned the reel.

"Ha ha!" The sound of his winning laughter merged with the frantic whisking of the reel and filled the bitter air. The old man pulled back with everything he had, leant forward and reeled, pulled back, leant forward and reeled. He repeated the series of moves over and over again with the verve and vigour of a much younger man, turning back the clock with every wind of the reel as hot blood thundered through his veins. The muscles in his arms cried out in pain but the old man didn't listen. He was in the zone and the adrenaline coursing through his nervous system drowned out all sounds. But it wasn't easy; the line fought back, tugging and cutting through the water in all directions as the old sea dog huffed and growled his way to a hard-fought victory. He couldn't remember the last time he'd locked horns with such a fish, such a beast. He couldn't wait to see exactly what he'd hooked and as he yanked and cranked and pulled and reeled, visions of monstrous cod and tope and eagle-like sting rays as wide as buses and conger eels as big as mythical serpents raced through his head. It was big, he was sure. Whatever it was, the old man knew it was a shoe-in for catch-of-the-day. Maybe even catch of the century.

"Bloody hell," he strained as the hungry reel gobbled

up another foot or two of the taught and jittering line.

"Looks like you little buggers are magic after all," he said, half-turning to the bucket of lucky ragworms... but there was nothing there. The bucket was empty. Lifeless. Clean. The old man did a double-take, then stopped.

"Wh-what?" he breathed, still gripping the rod and reel tight. He peered into the bottom of the bucket with a look of disbelief on his twisted, sweat-slicked face. There was nothing in there. Nothing but black plastic and a few beads of water. And then he felt the tension in his hands ease. The rod unclenched into a lifeless pole once more as the line relaxed, slackened. There was no weight. No resistance. No nothing.

"No," the old man whimpered, snapping his face back to the line. "Please, no." Tears of frustration formed and clouded his vision as he desperately reeled in a few more feet of limp line, unable to accept the fact that he'd squandered the biggest catch of his life no sooner than he'd found it. After maybe thirty seconds of frantic, fight-free reeling, the old man collapsed into his seat with a crushing sigh and put a hand to his brow. He'd blown it.

"Fuck," he spat through chattering teeth, pinching his forehead and cheek with a cold, arthritic claw that ached, now, from the pointless workout it had just been put through. He screwed his eyes shut and tried to picture what might have been, but the only thing his mind's eye could see was complete and utter blackness.

In the crestfallen silence, the old man's hand jabbed at his mind with pain. He heaved another dejected breath into his palm and spread it over his mouth and face. It was then that he suddenly became aware of two things: the fetid stench of rotten fish and the inexplicable stillness of the boat. He opened his eyes and looked up. The flat grey ocean stretched all around him, dead and quiet, its steady colour interrupted only by a scattering of phosphorus bubbles and the shadows cast by the dark clouds. They reached to the far horizons, to the fine pewter strip of the English Channel in front of him, to the dark gold slither of land behind where the horizon was lost in a still green mist, and the dark grey sky faded into the flat grey sea somewhere near the mainland. The silence was oppressive. And then:

"*Peeeeeeeetttteerrrrrrr...*"

His eyes widened.

"*Peeeeeeeetttteerrrrrrr...*"

He shook his head, refusing to acknowledge what he could hear loud and clear all around him. Then came a deep, crisp voice he knew all too well:

"Peter."

His heart stopped. What he felt was beyond the reach of words or horror. A deep, dark chill skittered over every last fibre in his aching body. His pale skin felt cold and infested as it broke out into gooseflesh. He caught his breath and slowly, tentatively, turned to face the empty bucket. Except it wasn't empty. Not anymore.

"Hello, Peter," the grotesque, severed head of his dead father croaked. "Long time, no see. How've you been? How's the missus?"

In his shock, the old man blinked in horror and shuffled back with an expression of amazement and pure revulsion.

"You're… you're..." He couldn't believe what his stricken eyes were showing him. His pulse soared and his tongue felt poisoned, swollen. The hideous scene was too much for him and hot vomit rushed up his throat and exploded from his mouth in a yellow spray.

"Oh dear," the ghoulish head crooned through skinless lips that were lined with gangrenous sores and crusty, off-white barnacles. The terrible, impossible cranium was nestled on a shifting bed of moist and clicking ragworms that writhed and oozed from the head's hollow eye sockets in maddening clumps and strings like severed entrails. The old man wanted to look away more than anything, but his eyes were glued to the ghastly face before him. A stillborn scream gurgled in the back of his burning throat.

"I've told you before, Peter," the eyeless head mocked, "there's nothing out here for you. Why do you keep doing this to yourself?"

"You're… you're… you're not real."

"Well, of course not," the head chuckled, "but in that fuzzy old head of yours I may as well be. So come on, why do you keep coming out here?"

"I… I… I…"

"Let me guess…" the head broke in, its mouth stretching back into a nightmarish grin to reveal a set of smashed grey teeth that were smothered in grit and bits of seaweed. An enormous, hissing worm bled from one of its gaping nostrils, trickling down its leathery philtrum and into its mouth. "…you forgot?"

The old man's jaw fell open in a look that was way beyond the realms of comprehension. He wanted to throw up all over again but something stopped him.

"*Tsk, tsk, tsk*. Oh, Peter," the head shook grotesquely, "how many times do I have to tell you—there's nothing out here for you. I know they say 'there's plenty more fish in the sea' but I think you've got the wrong end of the stick, old boy."

The old man struggled to catch his breath.

"I suppose it's all our fault in hindsight. Our generation… anyway, enough of all this Lovecraft nonsense. You best be on your way. Reel that sucker in and I'll see you in a few days." The head tilted itself in the direction of the old man's fallen rod which was violently shaking against the side of the boat. He tore his petrified gaze from the thing in the bucket and snatched the rod just before the sea could claim it. He snapped his head back to the bucket from Hell but the head was gone. All that remained was the squirming bed of ragworms—but there was something different about them. Their colour, their texture, their shine, sound and smell—it was all different. For some reason, the old man felt drawn to the bucket. Compelled to take a closer look, to inspect its fresh brand of gore. In the depths of his fear, he shuffled nervously towards the bucket, towards the hideous mirage. He swallowed hard and grimaced as a cocktail of acid and saliva burnt the back of his throat once more. And then he froze. For a second, he couldn't make out what he was—or wasn't—seeing, but then the realisation came crashing down on him like a ton of bricks. The bucket was full of wet, grey matter. Soft, churning tissue that glistened in its own terrible light. Brains. Human brains. The old man cried out in horror, stumbling back and away from the pulsing bucket.

"This isn't real," he moaned, clutching his trembling rod, "this… this—" and then the reel exploded into life like a possessed Geiger counter. Something large, powerful and hideously fast was making off with the line. The old man flinched at the ear-splitting sound and snapped his eyes to the grey sea once more, and then he saw it: a colossal ragworm the size of a train burst out of the water some thirty feet to the north, bending its grotesque, tube-like body into an enormous arc before crashing down and disappearing with a thunderous roar. The old man hurled the rod into the water and collapsed onto the engine with a whimper. He had never felt so frightened in his life. At least, not that his shattered memory would allow him to recall.

"*Peeeeeeeettttteerrrrrrr...*"

In his traumatised exhaustion, Peter Meredith crunched along the stony shore of the abandoned harbour, wiping what remained of the crusted vomit and tears from his cracked and quivering face.

"It's not real," he mumbled desperately to himself as he trudged, "it's not real." Through hot and stinging tears, he glanced to his right and spied two dark figures perched on a lonely bench that overlooked the shore. He put his head down, and walked on.

The two men sat half-drunk and huddled on the old bench with a carrier bag full of cheap beer between them. Upon seeing the old man stumble by, the taller of the two turned to his Thursday morning drinking buddy.

"Hold up, there he goes. Same batshit time, same batshit channel."

"You what?" The shorter, chubbier man looked up through beery eyes.

"Crazy Pete, look," he took a sip of his beer then

motioned towards the reeling old man. Speaking through a warm and gassy belch, he said, "Fuck me, look at him go!"

Disgusted, the shorter man replied: "Oh ease up, John, fuckin' hell mate."

"What?"

"You know what. Leave the old boy alone, would ya?"

The taller man twisted his face into a look of bewilderment but it was all an act. He knew what he was doing. "Bloody hell," he said, "who took the fish outta your fucking pie?"

"Nah, don't give me that, you shouldn't laugh, John. Geezer lost his wife last year and has bad Alzheimer's now apparently. Can happen to anyone."

The tall man recoiled. "I know, I know, I'm only having a laugh, Al, Jesus Christ mate."

The shorter man rolled his eyes and shook his head.

"Here," the tall man said, his speech slurred, "why'd they still let him go out there anyway? Ain't nobody told him?"

"Yeah," the short man nodded, "course they have. But some days he obviously forgets and before anyone can tell him he's already loaded all his gear onto his boat and he's out on the water, ain't he. You know how old people are with getting up early and stuff."

"Bloody hell. Surprised they ain't taken the boat off the poor bastard." He sniffed. "Well, you never know.

The old boy might bring us back something one of these days." He took another sip of his flat beer, "Christ, how long's it been now?"

"How long's what been?"

Grinning, the tall man raised his eyebrows and nudged his friend in the ribs, "You know what."

"Oh for fuck's sake."

"How long's it been, Alan? Come on. Remind your old pal, John."

"No."

"Go on."

"Such a wanker."

"I insist…"

The short man knew his irksome friend wouldn't let it go so he took the bait. "Gotta be at least four years now, I reckon."

"Four years?" the tall man crooned. "Has it really?"

"You bloody know how long it's been, Johnny."

"Oh, do I? And why's that, Alan my old chum?"

"Coz it was that fucking great big conger eel you caught off the pier. The last official, documented fish to be caught off the coast of Great Britain. January 20th, 2092."

"Ohhh, that's right," he said, slumping back into the cracked bench with a shit-eating grin on his red face, "must've slipped my mind."

"Wanker."

"Now, now, Alan, there's no need for that kinda

language. Besides, let's not write off the old man just yet," he raised his beer to the vague and drifting silhouette that was fading into the distance, like a ghost, "Life as we once knew it may be at the end of the line but, you never know—crazy Pete could still hook us a miracle."

There was a moment of quiet. An eerie, suffocating quiet that hung over the two drunks like an invisible, sobering blanket. The sound of the men's short, wheezing breaths merged with the moan of the wind and the splashing of low waves on the stony shore and then:

"Got more chance of catching bloody coronavirus these days than any fish."

The tall man snorted.

"Yeah, I know," he said, "Still can't believe they're all gone. If only old Pete could get his hands on some decent bait. Some magic rags, or somethin'."

"What the bloody hell are 'magic rags'?"

John Dory looked down at his feet and smiled faintly. "Never mind.

AUTHORS

Laurel Hightower

Laurel Hightower grew up in Kentucky, attending college in California and Tennessee before returning home to horse country, where she lives with her husband, son, and a rescue Pit bull. She works as a paralegal in a mid-size firm, wrangling litigators by day and writing at night. A bourbon and beer girl, she's a fan of horror movies and true life ghost stories.

She is the author of *Whispers in the Dark* and *Crossroads,* and co-edited the charity anthology *We Are Wolves* as well as *The Dead Inside,* an identity horror anthology. Her short fiction has appeared in several publications. *Below* is her third book.

Kay Hanifen

Kay Hanifen was born on a Friday the 13th and once lived for three months in a haunted castle. So, obviously, she had to become a horror writer.

Her articles have appeared in *Ghouls Magazine*, *Screen Rant*, *The Borgen Project*, and *Leatherneck* magazine; and her short stories have appeared in *Strangely Funny VIII*, *Crunchy With Ketchup*, *Midnight From Beyond the Stars*, *Dark Shadows: The Gay Nineties*, *Wicked Newsletters*, *Fearful Fun*, *Death of a Bad Neighbor*, *Enchanted Entrapments*, *Diet Riot: A Fatterpunk Anthology*, and *Slice of Paradise*.

When she's not consuming pop culture with the voraciousness of a vampire at a 24-hour blood bank, you can usually find her with her two black cats or on Twitter *@TheUnicornComi1*.

Joshua Marsella

Joshua Marsella is a Maine native. He lives with his wife, Aryn, and their two sons, Lucca and Lennon, in his hometown where he works as a stay-at-home dad.

Thus far he has written two ovellas, *Scratches* and *Severed*, his debut collection, *Hunger For Death,* several short stories in various anthologies, as well as contributing to the *FrightVision* middle grade horror series.

He has no plans to stop writing and looks forward to keeping his readers entertained for as long as he can.

Thomas Gloom

Thomas Gloom is an indie horror author, audiobook narrator, and host of the Into The Gloom podcast. He's a movie nerd, candle hoarder, and lover of all things spooky.

His latest novella is the deliciously addictive, eco-horror, revenge tale *The Potted Plant*, which features a witch, a flesh-eating plant, and plenty of blood!

He is always open to chatting with other horror fans, and the best places to connect with him are via email at *thomasgloom87@gmail.com* or on Instagram *@thomasgloom*.

MOCHA PENNINGTON

Mocha Pennington studied journalism with a minor in creative writing at college. Her recent shorts stories include "The Crimson Bride" featured in *Slash-Her*, an all female horror anthology from Kandisha Press and "Over The River and Through The Woods" featured in *Wild Violence* anthology via Blood Rites Horror.

She separates her time between writing her first novel and co-hosting Tea Time, a gossip channel on YouTube, which has accumulated over a million views.

Don't be scared to follow her:

Twitter: *@Mocha_Writer*
Instagram: *@MochaPenn*
YouTube: *youtube.com/c/teatimexoxo*

Nicola Kapron

Nicola Kapron has previously been published by *Neo-opsis Science Fiction Magazine,* Rebel Mountain Press, Soteira Press, *All Worlds Wayfarer*, Mannison Press, and more.

Nicola lives in Nanaimo, British Columbia, with a hoard of books—mostly fantasy and horror—and an extremely fluffy cat.

Nikki R. Leigh

Nikki R. Leigh is a queer forever-90s kid wallowing in all things horror. When not writing horror fiction and poetry, she can be found creating custom horror-inspired toys, making comics, and hunting vintage paperbacks. She reads her stories to her partner and her cat, one of which gets scared very easily.

Instagram: *@spinetinglers*
Twitter: *@fivexxfive*

Website: *spinetinglershorror.com*
Email: *spinetinglersmedia@gmail.com*

SPENCER HAMILTON

Spencer Hamilton is a queer author living in Philadelphia. His debut short story collection and novel, *Kitchen Sink* and *The Fear*, were published in 2020.

His short fiction has appeared in various anthologies from publishers such as Blood Rites Horror, DarkLit Press, and Dead Sea Press.

His latest release, the novella *Sister Funtime*, is the first in a series set in his Smileyland universe. You can download the free novella *Welcome to Smileyland* by joining his newsletter at *SpencerHamiltonBooks.com.*

Twitter: *@SHamiltonBooks*
Instagram: *@spencer.hamilton.books*

Matthew Stevens

Matthew Stevens spent years dreaming about being a writer before finding time to begin creating characters and worlds and the stories for them to inhabit. His current projects find him dabbling in a wide range of genres. He is currently working on a fantasy novella and numerous sci-fi and horror shorts, along with an occasional blog post examining his perspective on his own writing journey and any intriguing geeky topic that catches his attention.

He can be found online at:

Facebook: *facebook.com/matthewstevensauthor*
Twitter: *@matt_the_writer*
Blog: *theedgeofeverything.wordpress.com*

MEGAN KIEKEL ANDERSON

Megan Kiekel Anderson loves the stranger-than-fiction creatures of the deep ocean and was excited to expand her knowledge for this anthology. She is an emerging poet, short story writer, and novelist from Kansas City. She earned her undergraduate degree in sociology from Park University.

You can find her on Instagram: *@Megan_NerdNest*

Andrew Cull

Andrew Cull is an award-winning writer and horror director.

He's the author of *Bones*, *Remains*, and, most recently, *The Cockroach King*. His story collection *Bones* has been described as "a masterclass in emotional cinematic horror fiction."

Andrew lives in Melbourne, Australia. He loves horror and Hitchcock, and, like you, he's not easily scared.

Follow Andy on Twitter: *@andrewcull*

Catarina Prata

Catarina Prata is a Portuguese writer, whose life has always been filled with books.

Currently pursuing a PhD in Cognitive and Affective Neurosciences, at Porto University, she loves to dabble in horror and fantasy, reading and writing stories. She is also a book reviewer and fights for a responsible and pertinent exploration of mental health in stories.

“The Last Dive” is her first story written in English, but she believes many more are to come.

Hannah Hulbert

Hannah Hulbert is a full-time mum and part-time writer from the south coast of England. She enjoys looking for mushrooms, doing crafts, and drinking tea, especially when she is supposed to be writing.

You can find her stories in *Metaphorosis*, *Lunar Station Quarterly* and the anthology *Cat Ladies of the Apocalypse*, among others. Her story "Ruler of Waves, God of Trees" from *Growth* (TL;DR Press, 2021), received a Pushcart nomination.

Craig Wallwork

Craig Wallwork is the three times nominated Pushcart author of the Tom Nolan detective series including *Bad People* and *Labyrinth of the Dolls*. He is also the author of the novels *The Sound of Loneliness* and *Heart of Glass*, as well as the short story collections, *Gory Hole*, *Quintessence of Dust*, and *Human Tenderloin*. He lives in Yorkshire, England.

You can find out more about Craig and his books on his website: *www.craigwallwork.com*

Jack Harding

Jack was born and raised in Portsmouth, United Kingdom.

His favourite authors are Ray Bradbury, Richard Matheson, Alan Moore and Stephen King. His favourite books are *The Illustrated Man, I Am Legend, From Hell,* and *The Dead Zone.*

Jack's debut short story collection, *Ripper Country*, is available to purchase through Amazon and Blood Rites Horror Publishing. He is the author of many short horror stories which can be found across a number of published anthologies. He is currently putting the finishing touches on his second collection of short stories, *Dark Lines,* which features the acclaimed self-published tales, "React" and "Driving in the Dark". The collection is set for publication through DarkLit Press later in 2022.

Find him on Instagram: *@rocket.man.reads*

Acknowledgements

I would like to thank pretty much everybody I know for making this possible. Firstly, of course, the fifteen fantastic authors who featured in this book; but also every single person who submitted a story, who wrote and worked and proved their passion and love for the anthology and the cause it means to support. I do hope you'll keep sending me stories as we make more and more books.

To every single person who's dedicated their time and money to reading this: thank you. Your profits are going to a good place, and hopefully so did your fear-loving brain for a little while. Please do look out for the next books in the *Dead Seas* series and make everyone you know aware that they need to do just the same!

To The Shark Trust, for indulging me, and for everything you do to protect the ocean and its beautiful, misunderstood and wonderful creatures.

And as always, thank you to my partner, Emily, without whom I would have lost the will to do any of this a long time ago.

ABOUT THE SHARK TRUST

The Shark Trust is a UK-based charitable organisation working toward the protection and conservation of sharks, skates and rays. They do this in a number of ways, including educating, enforcing positive change through campaigns for species protection and responsible trade, and influencing fisheries and organisations to do better.

Every penny of profit from sales of this book goes to The Shark Trust, but you can also donate or find out more by visiting *sharktrust.org*

Thank you for your support!

Content Warnings

Read on for details of any potentially upsetting content that may appear in the stories in this book. Please be aware these warnings may contain spoilers.

While I've tried to be as comprehensive as possible, please do let me know if I've missed something at *deadseapress@gmail.com*. Thank you.

In all/most stories:
Violence and graphic descriptions. Death and injury of adult characters. Potentially strong language. Threat of drowning.

In *The Angler and the Raven*:
Death (mentioned) of multiple children.

In *Melancholic Blue*:
Mentions of domestic abuse, both verbal and physical.

In *Werewolves and Tentacles*:
Death (mentioned) of a sibling.

In *Julia*:
Death of a child, grief, mentions and evidence of self-harm.

In *The Last Dive*:
Mentions of domestic unrest.

In *Pressure Differentials*:
Claustrophobia.

In *The Many Ghosts of the Deep*:
Threat to and potential death of children, plane crash.

MORE FROM DEAD SEA PRESS

DEAD SEAS VOLUME II
SHADOWS BENEATH THE SURFACE
AN ANTHOLOGY OF AQUATIC HORROR

VOLUME III
DEATH IN THE DEEP
AN ANTHOLOGY OF AQUATIC HORROR
EDITED BY JAY ALEXANDER

RAMPAGE ON THE REEFS

Coming June 13th

HORROR ON THE HOOK

Coming July 13th

DEVILS ON THE DECK

Coming August 13th

FEAR IN THE FROZEN WATERS

Coming this Christmas

RUN FROM THE RIVER

Coming early 2023